ROPER RETURNS

J. ALSPAUGH

Dedication

To my siblings who have stuck with me through the good times and the bad. Thank you for always being willing to speak the truth in love.

Jason Roper Book Series

ONE

"Name?"

"Jason Roper"

"Age?"

"Nineteen, I'll be twenty next month."

"Your records show your birthday is in August." The elderly man looked at Jason over his reading glasses.

Jason frowned. "Yes, Sir. There was a mix up on that. My birthday is in April."

The man looked at him skeptically. "That's a pretty big mix up."

Jason nodded. "I'm working on straightening it out."

"Hmm." The man stared at him for a minute longer, then went back to the papers before him. "Day?"

"Oh, Um, April 30th."

He pulled his reading glasses off and tapped them on the paper. "This says you were born on the 15th."

"I know." Jason met his eyes. "I told you, there was a mix up."

"We pride ourselves on the accuracy of our records."

"Well, Sir. The information you have is obviously outdated." Jason glanced out the front window at Benjamin who gave him a warning look and tapped his wrist to remind Jason time was passing.

"Your birth date is not something that gets outdated." The man countered.

"Yeah, that's interesting, but I need to renew my license. Can't you just copy the information off this one?" Jason held up his expired license.

"No, I'm afraid not. You could have forged it for all I know."

"Look, I'm just trying to be legal. I don't know how the dates got swapped but I can assure you that I, Jason Roper, was born on April 30th." Jason turned away, giving himself a minute to cool off. He was certain his dad was behind it. Once his hero work had crossed with his dad's plans, their relationship was over. It was his dad, Nathan McCard, who had gotten him his new identity. He had told Jason that renewing the license after a year would make it officially legal since it would then be issued by a government agency.

Apparently, McCard had covered his tracks too well, or else he could have simply exposed Jason's identity as a fraud. But somehow, before he was taken by the police, McCard had managed to change Jason's birthdate in the system. August 15th was the only day Jason's dad believed his son could lose his invincibility. Jason could only assume his dad was trying to make it easier for people to discover his "weakness". That had been Jason's birthday before, but that was when he had been Patrick McCard. He was Jason Roper now, and could never go back. Patrick had died for good when his father turned out to be the leader of the gang Jason had helped to destroy. Jason wondered how many other things his dad had changed before they hauled him off to prison.

"Are you going to finish this?" The thin man was clearly annoyed.

"Yes, I'm sorry." Jason took a deep breath and turned to face him. "What else do you need?"

"I'll need to see your old license again."

"The birth date is right on it." Jason pointed it out as he handed it across to the man.

"Hmm." He studied it and then Jason before scribbling

down some information onto his paper. "Stand over there." He pointed to a white screen and Jason obeyed.

"What's taking you so long?" Benjamin asked coming through the door. "We have places to be, man."

"I can't issue you a license here," the man told Benjamin matter-of-factly. "You have a record."

"You already told me that." Benjamin put his hands up in dramatized submission. "Do I look like I'm asking? Just renew his and let us leave."

"He's got to take my picture and I'm out of here. Five minutes max."

The man gave them a knowing look over his glasses.

"Hey, wait." Jason went back to the counter. "Give my license back."

"I need to check something."

"No. You need to return it," Jason retorted firmly. "An expired license is better than no license, your records are screwy and right now that's my only proof."

The man rose, his movements calculated as he started for the door behind him.

Benjamin sprang over the counter and stepped into his path. He was at least a foot and a half taller than the clerk. "I think my friend said he'd rather you didn't run off with his license."

The man's eyes grew wide. "You're not allowed…"

"I'd give it to him," Jason advised. "Remember, he's got a record."

———

"What's on your record anyway?" Jason asked. The Mustang beeped as they approached.

Benjamin shrugged at him over the top of the car. "Beats me. Maybe I killed someone or something." He ducked out of sight as he slid into the passenger seat.

Jason put the key into the ignition then looked over at Benjamin. "Did you kill someone?"

Benjamin laughed. "Afraid you have a psycho killer on your hands?"

"That would make an odd combination."

Benjamin grinned and ran his hand out in front of him as if tracing a headline. "Hero chooses psycho killer for sidekick." He glanced over at Jason and saw he was still waiting for an answer. "Nah, I didn't kill anyone. I might have roughed a few up in my time, but never took a life." He looked at Jason. "Happy?"

Jason shrugged and put the car in gear. "It's good to know."

"So now we go to that little lakeside slum and save the world?" Benjamin asked as they cruised down the street.

Jason glanced at him. "Something like that."

"Have you heard any more about the case?"

"No, just what I told you." Jason kept his eyes on the road. "Is the curiosity killing you?"

"Hey, luck favors the prepared," Benjamin answered pulling the letter from between the seats.

"I don't believe in luck."

"Have it your way." Benjamin shrugged. "I bet God likes it when you are prepared, less for Him to do."

Jason rolled his eyes. "Benjamin, you're a nut."

"And proud of it. Now let's see…" he glanced over the letter. "Your mission is…?"

"Our mission," Jason corrected. "Is to find out where 'person one' hid something. And we are to do this by getting someone named Territ to spill what he knows."

"Territ is such a strange name," Benjamin interjected.

"Maybe it is short for something," Jason told him nonchalantly.

"You said that before." Benjamin folded the letter and stuck it back between the seats. "There is nothing for it to be short for."

Jason laughed. "Well then stop saying it's strange. If the kid's parents wanted to name him that I guess there wasn't much he could do about it."

"I guess you're right. But he could have changed his name."

"Maybe he likes it, Benjamin. When you have a kid, name him something else."

"I will," Benjamin told him emphatically.

"What gets me is why the FBI didn't give us the name of the person who was hiding the big secret thing, the one who died. I mean wouldn't it be helpful for us to know who it was?"

"Unless we do know him, or did." Benjamin added thoughtfully.

"Well, whoever he was, he apparently got shot down and only told this Territ guy where he hid whatever it was. That's the other thing, what's the big secret? Did he have some national secret, or the plans for a weapon or something?" Jason glanced over his shoulder as they merged onto the interstate.

"So Taroe is not connected with this case?" Benjamin asked.

"The man who gave me the message said someone named Bartlett would fill us in when we arrived. He said we would just have to ask when we get there." Jason shook his head. "I like working with Taroe better. He is a lot better about filling us in."

"What could happen? You're invincible, and we've got these babies to back us up." Benjamin grinned, pulling out his hand gun.

Jason laughed. "We probably should ask some questions before we go around shooting things."

Benjamin shrugged. "I guess we'll figure it out when the time comes."

T WO

"Hi, I'm Thomas Bartlett." The man was short and wide. His dark hair was meticulously combed and his face serious behind his smile.

"Good to meet you, Mr. Bartlett." Jason shook the man's hand. "I'm Roper. And this is my colleague, Benjamin Curr."

Benjamin grinned. He had just been promoted to Jason's "colleague" and he liked the sound of it.

Bartlett hesitated. "I wasn't aware you had a partner."

Jason shrugged. "Benjamin comes with the deal. He goes where I go. Think of it as a bonus."

"Pleasure." Benjamin extended his hand and Bartlett shook it out of politeness.

"Mr. Bartlett, there are a few questions we'd like to ask you before we meet Territ," Jason told him.

"I'd be happy to answer any questions you have. My office is just this way."

"Thank you."

They followed him down a long hall and into a plush office. He gestured to the leather chairs and took his place behind his big desk. "I am sorry the message was so cryptic. I heard about you through someone who knows Taroe. Since you are working for yourself and I knew nothing about your level of security clearance I wanted to be careful with how much information I gave you. Taroe assures me that you can be trusted with this mission."

"The information you gave us was very vague. Naturally we will need to know a bit more before we sign on."

"Naturally." Bartlett folded his wide hands on his desk.

"First we'd like to know the name of the man who was killed."

"His name was Toby."

Benjamin stiffened and his eyes locked on Bartlett. "Toby who? What was his last name?" Benjamin's face was hard and emotionless.

"Toby Black. Did you know him?" Bartlett's tone was innocent.

"Alright drop it."

"Drop what?"

"The act," Benjamin told him bluntly. "You work for the FBI, right?"

"Not exactly. This is more of a side branch."

"Well, the FBI has told you a lot more than you are letting on. You requested us by name. You know who he is." Benjamin jerked his thumb at Jason. "And you know who I am. You knew we both knew Toby before you asked us to be assigned to this case. You level with us or we'll walk right back out and let you deal with it."

Bartlett was unshaken by the outburst. He turned his attention to Jason. "Does he always react like this?"

"Toby was an... acquaintance of ours. We were not aware that he had passed away," Jason answered calmly. "If we are going to be any help to you, you will need to give us all the information you have about Toby's death."

Bartlett nodded. "We had trouble with...activity in the slums ever since you broke up the Jarris gang. People coming and going, a lot of hush-hush activity going on under the radar. There was a very important document stolen from an agent of ours. Toby was mixed up with the group responsible for the theft. Toby Black was the last known possessor of the information, but someone else got a hold of him before we did. We knew he was transporting the information, but he shook the man tailing him and we did not reach the body until several minutes after he was shot. By that time Territ had already concealed what Toby was transporting."

"Did you shoot him?" Benjamin asked pointedly.

Bartlett looked startled. "We were trailing him to see who he was passing the information to, not hunting him. Territ is the only one who knows where that document is hidden. It is vital that we get the document before the other side gets to it."

Jason nodded thoughtfully. "Who exactly is Territ?"

"Territ is Toby's son, his eldest." Bartlett smiled. "Does that surprise you? I guess you didn't think a man like Toby would have a family."

"We knew he had a family," Benjamin informed him coolly. "Get on with it. How old is Territ?"

"Territ is sixteen."

"He's a little young isn't he?" Jason asked. "Is it legal for you to hold him?"

"The information he is withholding makes his safety vital. There are people from his father's…I'll use the term "gang" for lack of another word, although it is more complicated than the Jarris thing was. We have had him here for several weeks but he refuses to give us any information."

"That's not a surprise," Benjamin muttered.

Jason rose. "Will you excuse us for a moment?"

Benjamin followed Jason into the hall and Jason shut the door behind them.

"What's the deal, Benjamin?" Jason demanded in a low voice. "The man's just trying to fill us in and you are tearing into him every chance you get."

"He's a snake, Jason." Benjamin's eyes were hard. "What he's saying about Toby is not true."

"Maybe Toby wasn't all you thought he was," Jason replied, the irritation gone from his voice.

Benjamin looked at him without responding. The hardness in Benjamin's features reminded Jason of when Benjamin was working with Toby in the gang. It worried him to see how easily that shell had come between them.

"Let's go back in and hear him out." Jason broke the silence.

Benjamin nodded but Jason could see he was not convinced.

Jason pushed the office door open and let Benjamin enter first. "Thank you for your patience."

"Not a problem, I did not realize you had not read about Toby's death. I'm sure it came as a shock."

Jason was glad Bartlett had decided to take a kinder approach.

They took their seats once more and Bartlett leaned back in his chair.

"As I was saying, we have had Territ for almost a month now and have tried everything short of torture to get him to talk."

"So where do we come in?" Jason asked.

"We've used adults to question him, to befriend him in hopes that he would share the information with them. He simply denies the fact that he knows anything about it. So we thought if we brought someone closer to his age, and who had some connection with his father we might get what we are after."

"What if he really doesn't know?" Jason asked calmly.

"Jason, if you…"

"I prefer Roper, if you don't mind."

"He prefers it even if you do." Benjamin was rewarded by a quick silencing glare from Jason.

"Roper it is then," Bartlett said with an amused smile. "As I was saying, if you had been there and seen his face when he stood up from beside the body..."

"It was his dad, you moron," Benjamin lashed out. "Of course he was going to have a strange look. Have you ever seen someone you love die in a gutter? It does things to you."

"I can tell," Bartlett answered. His patience was wearing thin.

"Mr. Bartlett" Jason leaned forward. "What exactly is it you are after?"

Bartlett shifted in his seat causing the springs to groan in protest. "I'm not at liberty to disclose that information. All I can tell you is it is vital that we get it back."

"How are we supposed to know if he tells us?"

"You'll know. Besides we have his quarters bugged so we will pick up on it if he says anything."

"What a pain." Benjamin got up and walked to the book-case. "Can you imagine someone eavesdropping on you 24/7? All these books could be bugged for all we know."

"Don't be ridiculous, Mr. Curr."

Jason frowned. "So basically you want Benjamin and I to get all chummy with this kid and then squeeze the secret out of him?"

"That's correct."

"That's kind of heartless," Jason continued. "Like a planned out betrayal."

"You don't have to paint it so black you know," Bartlett told him. "The kid has something that could endanger a lot of lives if it gets into the wrong hands. We want to get it before they do."

"Alright, let's see him. After I talk with him I'll decide if I'll take your case."

"You certainly are a businesslike 'hero', Roper. I hope we can get along."

"I guess we'll see." Jason rose. "Where do I find Territ?"

THREE

"I'll leave you to get acquainted," Bartlett told them and hurried off down the hall.

"He probably wants to get behind the monitors and watch your act," Benjamin told him.

Jason smiled for Benjamin's sake. This was all happening too fast. He needed time to think, to sort it out and formulate a plan. He knocked gently on the door.

"Go away."

Jason pushed the door open slowly. "Can we come in?"

"No." Territ was sitting on a couch across the room with his arms folded stubbornly. He was dark and thin like his father had been. The resemblance was amazingly accurate. He glared at them, his deep brown eyes drilling into them.

Jason hesitated before entering. "Why not?"

"Because I don't want you in here," Territ told him bluntly. "I don't want any of your fake friendship or prying questions."

"He's pretty smart." Benjamin liked him already.

Jason went in, letting Benjamin shut the door behind them. "I guess you know why we are here."

"Yes." Territ was still glaring. "You knew my father and wanted to befriend his orphaned son."

"What about your mother?" Benjamin asked plopping himself on the couch. "And all your brothers and sisters?"

"What do you know about it?" Territ asked defensively.

"I just remember Toby having more than one kid," Benjamin answered.

"You might as well drop it. I know you just got it all from Bartlett and his goons."

"What are his goons like?" Jason asked. He saw Territ relax just a little.

"A bunch of ruffians, same as any other crook has."

"Hmm. He didn't tell us about that."

"Why would he?" Territ asked. "He's just trying to get you to believe his story."

"What is his story?"

"Oh, you're very clever," Territ responded. "That was a nice round about way to get to the subject."

"Lay off man," Benjamin told him. "Relax a little. We're here to help you, not throw you in the slammer."

"Getting all ghetto isn't going to make me talk," Territ told him.

Benjamin sat up. "Hey, I'm not ghetto." He looked at Jason. "Right?"

Jason did not answer. "Territ, is your room always bugged?"

Territ looked startled.

"Is there anywhere we could talk without being overheard?"

"You certainly get to the point, now don't you?" Territ observed. "I'm not supposed to know about that."

"But you do." Jason looked around the room. There was a kitchenette on the other side and a little table with a few chairs around it. The open area they were in served as a living room and was equipped with two couches to seat his many guests. A door to Territ's right probably led to his bedroom.

"What if I do?" Territ was waiting.

Jason pulled one of the chairs over and sat. "If I was under constant surveillance I think I would…shake the system."

"What do you mean?" The accusing glare was gone.

"Find a place I could be alone, or an escape or something," Jason answered. "I'm guessing if you are anything like your dad, you already know where the bugs are."

Territ gave him a little crooked smile in answer.

"Are you under surveillance as well?"

"I don't see what that has to do with anything," Territ told him, his tone was disinterested again.

Jason smiled. "Alright, I'll let it go."

Territ pointed to a decorative plant on the coffee table.

Jason gave Benjamin a cue with his eyes and then approached the plant.

"So," Benjamin spoke up. "Do you have any hobbies?"

"No," Territ answered watching Jason as he peered between the plastic leaves.

"You must have some kind of hobby." Benjamin urged. He mouthed. "Come on"

"Well, I like to walk."

Benjamin stifled a laugh. "That's an interesting hobby."

Territ glared at him. "You're the one who asked."

Jason pulled something from the plant and laid it on the table.

"Next?" he mouthed.

"So you like to walk?" Benjamin continued his monologue. "I enjoy walking too."

Territ took Jason to the next bug and in five minutes there were three lying on the table.

"In fact, walking has been proven to enhance your overall health. Did you know that?" Benjamin went on with a grin, trying to sound interested.

Jason laid the last bug on the table and before Territ could object he pulled out his Glock. With quick powerful strokes Jason smashed each one with the butt of his gun.

"You're not supposed to have that!" Territ told him, his eyes fearful.

"Yeah, well sometimes I don't obey all the rules," Jason told him motioning to the door.

Benjamin grabbed one of the kitchen chairs and wedged the back under the door knob. "We have about three minutes max."

"We're here to help you. Whatever it is, we can help with it. Your father was a friend of ours and we are going to do everything we can to get to the bottom of this."

Territ's eyes narrowed.

"Listen, we will need some time to find out who killed your dad. We want you to keep stalling them."

"I don't know what you're talking about."

"Yeah, sure. Just keep it up. We'll get around and talk to people and get a better grasp of what happened. Then we'll take it from there. You just keep that document out of their hands until we can get whoever it is who wants it."

Territ looked like he would have spoken but the sound of heavy footsteps silenced him once more.

"What, Territ? What were you going to say?" Jason asked urgently.

Someone tried the door and then pushed against it.

Territ shook his head, a glimmer of fear in his eyes. "Nothing."

"Man, you got to level with us," Benjamin hissed as the person on the other side of the door pushed harder.

Territ had closed up again and Jason knew it was no use to coax him. He nodded to Benjamin who, as soon as the pressure on the door let up, jerked the chair from under the knob and swung it around to its place by the table. The door flew open and several men in suits burst into the room. "What's going on?" one demanded, his eyes coming to rest on the scraps of metal on the table. "What's the meaning of this?"

"We were just trying to get him to talk," Jason told him as if he were surprised at the invasion. "I thought if we took the bugs away for a bit he'd feel a little more free to talk."

The man looked him over. "Don't do anything without

checking it by Bartlett," he told them sternly. "I think you've had long enough to get acquainted."

"Jerks," Territ muttered.

"It's your fault you're here, buddy," The man told him harshly "You can leave whenever you want to let us in on your little secret."

"I don't know anything about it," Territ muttered. "Get your spies out of here."

The man looked as if he might strike Territ. One of the other men touched his arm. "Someday." He warned making a fist and holding it up between himself and the boy.

"Come on." The men escorted Jason and Benjamin out of the room.

FOUR

Benjamin pulled the car door shut and Jason started the motor.

"What do you think?"

Benjamin shrugged. "Seems like a good kid."

"I mean about Bartlett and all of it," Jason clarified, glancing over at him.

Benjamin shrugged again. "I wasn't real keen on Bartlett, but it's your decision."

"Why's that?"

"You're the hero. He wanted you, not me." Benjamin smiled "I did like being a colleague though."

"That's what you are," Jason answered. "A sidekick works for the main guy, you don't work for me, you work with me."

Benjamin was silent.

"What's the matter?"

"I don't know," Benjamin looked out the side window as he talked. "I guess I don't really want to do this."

"This mission, or work with me?" Jason asked.

"The mission mostly," Benjamin answered. "I was close to Toby, I don't feel right about turning on his family."

"We're not turning on them," Jason reminded him stopping at a red light. "We're helping him. I meant what I said about getting to the bottom of it all, even if Bartlett is at the bottom."

"What if Toby was?" Benjamin asked.

The light turned green and Jason pushed the gas. "I guess I'd have to deal with it."

"See, you're a hero. You have to do what's right and save all the little hurting people. But I don't. It's optional for me."

"Not really. God tells everyone to help the hurting, He doesn't say anything about having super powers to do it. Other than His power."

"Yeah, that's all good for you. I knew when we got here you were going to take the case. It's like any superhero, they have to come when people need them. They don't have a choice. Bartlett called for help and here you are."

"You're here too," Jason reminded him.

"Yeah." Benjamin shifted uncomfortably.

"What was the hotel address again?" Jason asked.

"246 North Murell," Benjamin told him.

"Thanks."

They were silent as Jason maneuvered through the streets. He pulled into the hotel parking lot and shut off the engine. Benjamin opened his door but shut it again when Jason made no move to get out.

"You knew Toby lived here," Jason said quietly. "That's why you came."

Benjamin did not answer.

"You could have told me," Jason said after a while. "I would have let you come. You didn't have to pretend you were coming to help me."

"I didn't have a way to get here," Benjamin confessed.

Jason ran his fingers through his hair. "I just wish you had told me."

Benjamin did not meet his eyes.

"You were just going to live off me, and stay in the complementary hotel room?"

"No," Benjamin muttered. "I was going to find my own place to stay once we got here. I can pay for part of the gas if that will make you feel better."

Jason gripped the top of the steering wheel. "It's not that." He looked over at Benjamin. "I don't know what it is. I guess I never really thought this far ahead." He smiled weakly. "I should have known you couldn't just hang out with me forever. You have a life of your own."

Benjamin nodded. He knew this was tearing Jason up, but it had to be done. Sure, Jason had saved his life, but Benjamin had repaid his debt by helping him clear out the Jarris gang. He had even accompanied him on the mission Taroe had given them. Benjamin had already told Jason, Toby was off limits. This was something he needed to do and he knew if he was stuck to Jason he would never get it done. Pushing open his door, Benjamin stepped out.

"Will you pop the trunk?"

Jason pressed the button.

Benjamin closed his door and went to get his bag out of the trunk.

Jason put his hand on the top of the steering wheel and rested his head on it. He took a deep breath and let it out slowly. "Lord help me to deal with this," he whispered. He waited a moment longer then pushed open the driver's door.

"I can drive you someplace," Jason told Benjamin.

"That's okay, I'll find a place. Sometimes they charge more if you have a snazzy car." Benjamin shouldered his backpack and glanced at Jason. "I guess that's all. Good luck on your case. Or God bless or whatever."

Jason smiled weakly and offered his hand. "Thanks for everything."

"Sure." Benjamin shook his hand. "Take care."

Jason watched him go. He tried to tell himself it was better not to have Benjamin with him because that way he didn't have anyone to worry about, but he suddenly felt intensely alone. His dad was in prison, his mom was dead, and his only friend was walking off to disappear into the slums. "I guess it's just You and me, Lord," he said aloud.

He felt someone watching him and looked toward the street out of the corner of his eye. A small dark haired boy stood looking at him from the sidewalk.

Jason turned to look at him and frowned. "You're Territ's brother aren't you?"

The boy's eyes grew wide and he took off.

Jason slammed his trunk and raced after him catching the boy a block away. "Wait, buddy. I'm not going to hurt you."

The little boy struggled to get away.

"Listen." Jason tried to keep his hold on the squirming boy. "Hey, stop it. I just want to ask you a question."

"I'm not allowed to talk to you," the boy said through clenched teeth, still endeavoring to free himself.

"You don't even know who I am," Jason protested.

"You're one of those men who took Territ away."

"No, I'm not."

The boy paused to look at Jason. "How come you know him?"

"I…"

"See, I told you," The boy crowed when Jason hesitated. "You are."

"No, I'm not. Just sit down." Jason pulled him over to the steps of what looked like the town hall. He put a finger through the boy's belt loop and pulled him down on to the curb. "You going to stay?" Jason asked. He didn't trust the crafty look he saw in the boy's eyes.

"Yeah."

"Okay." Jason let go. "Now…"

The boy leapt to his feet and raced across the street. A car honked and screeched its tires as he crossed in front of it. The driver yelled at him, but the boy raced on. Jason groaned and took up the chase. They wove through the streets, and the houses quickly grew more and more run-down. As they entered a dilapidated apartment complex, a big man yelled at Jason as he passed, not bothering to get out of his dirty lawn chair. The boy led Jason in several circles around the complex and finally stopped to catch his breath.

"Why you chasin' me?" he asked breathlessly.

Jason bent and rested his hands on his knees, breathing heavily. "Man, you can run, kid."

The boy looked pleased. "I'm the fastest in my neighborhood."

"I bet you are."

"Sammis, who's that with you?" a girl called from the porch of one of the apartments.

"Don't know," Sammis yelled back. "He was chasin' me."

That caused a stir in the house and soon a boy who was about the same height as the girl appeared with a little girl tagging along behind. They approached him cautiously, accompanied by the girl from the porch.

"Who are you?" the girl asked suspiciously. "We don't like strangers around here."

"I can see that." Jason grinned and straightened up. "I'm a friend of your father's."

"Daddy died," Sammis informed him seriously.

"I know. I was coming to see if there was anything I could do for you guys while they are holding Territ. I saw him today. He's doing good. Seems like he wanted to be home, though."

"Why don't you let him go then?" the older boy asked accusingly.

"I'm not in charge of him. See, I came to help him out but I don't have any authority to let him go."

"Yeah, right. You got him trapped up there and are monitoring everything he says."

"They do," Jason corrected. "I'm here to help, but I have to learn out more about what happened before I can do anything. You guys can help."

"Yeah, right," The boy repeated. "You're not fooling anyone."

"You go tell your boss that we're not falling for it," the girl told him. "We're sick of you guys prying into our privacy."

"You're not allowed in our house," The little girl informed him seriously. Jason guessed she was around four.

"Hannah, be quiet," her sister commanded.

Hannah meekly obeyed.

"We don't need your help," the older boy told Jason firmly. "We're fine." He couldn't have been more than fourteen years old, but he held his chin high and spoke to Jason like a man.

"So they have your house bugged as well?" Jason asked him seriously.

"No, and if you try to bug it again..." the girl shot back.

"That's not your business," the boy informed him, cutting short his sister's threat. His sister took the little girl's hand, trying to herd Sammis back into the house.

"Are you going to stay?" the little girl asked shyly as the older girl pulled her toward the house.

"No, he's not," her sister told her.

"I might stick around and wait for your mother to come home," Jason told her. He was rewarded by a shy smile.

"My mother doesn't want to see you."

"Stop being so bossy, Rouwa," Sammis told her. "Mom won't mind talking to him."

Rouwa glared at him. "You don't know anything. Go inside, all of you."

"No," Sammis objected. He looked up at Jason. "What's your name?"

"Roper," Jason replied.

"Roper," Rouwa repeated softly. Jason could tell she was thinking hard.

"Yes."

"I've heard that name before."

Jason met her eyes. "You probably have. Give it some thought." He turned to the other kids. "Now let me see if I can get you all straight. Territ is sixteen and you must be the second born." Jason pointed at the older boy. He hadn't heard a name for him yet. "I'd say you're about fourteen?"

"Yep." Sammis wanted him to keep going. "Except Raquel's third not second."

"Sammis." There was a warning in her tone and he let it go.

Jason didn't press the subject. He had found out what he needed to know. There was another child, whether older or younger than Territ he didn't know. "Rouwa's next... I'd say you're...twelve."

She didn't respond.

Jason turned to the boy he had followed. "And you're Sammis." Jason stroked his chin thoughtfully. "By the looks of you I'd say you were eight."

"Nope, I just turned nine," Sammis told him proudly.

"Wow, congratulations." Jason looked around and spotted the little girl behind Raquel.

"And you're the last one?" he asked her.

She gave him her shy smile and held up four fingers.

"You're four?! Wow."

Hannah giggled.

"So now you know all about us," Raquel observed begrudgingly.

"Now it's our turn," Rouwa told him stepping forward. The others looked a little surprised. "Do you have any siblings?"

"No." Jason replied truthfully.

"How about your parents?" Raquel pressed.

Jason hesitated. "My mom died."

"And your dad?" Sammis pressed.

"That's my silent answer," Jason told them.

"What does that mean?" Sammis asked.

"It means I don't have to answer it."

"Is he dead?"

Jason looked down. He wished his dad were dead. Jason could not seem to forgive him for all the years of lies. "No."

"So your dad's a criminal or something," Raquel decided.

"There you go, now you know about me." Jason ignored Raquel's observation.

"Not much," Rouwa complained.

"You know as much as I do about you," Jason told her.

"Let's play question, question." Sammis grabbed Jason's arm and led him to a grassy patch in the lawn. "Sit here."

Jason obeyed, sitting cross legged in the grass. He didn't have to be anywhere until the morning and his room was already reserved for the night. Sammis and Hannah, who had broken away from Rouwa's grip, sat in front of him, while the older two drifted over to watch.

"Now what?"

"The rules are we ask a question and you have to answer it, then you ask and we answer," Sammis told him. "We go first."

"Okay." Jason picked a blade of grass, stretched out his legs and leaned back with his hands clasped behind his head. "Shoot."

"How old are you?" Sammis asked imitating Jason's position.

"Nineteen," Jason answered.

"Your turn."

"Um...Where's your mother?"

"Shopping," Sammis replied.

"Where were you born?" Rouwa asked quickly.

Jason squinted up at her. "That's a complicated one."

"Why?"

He sat up a little supporting himself with his elbow. "Well, I was born as one person, then that person sort of died and now I'm who I am now."

"Huh?"

"So you always were, like God?" Sammis was impressed. Jason laughed. "No."

"He changed his name, Sammis," Raquel explained coolly.

"You can ask a new one," Jason told them lying back again. This was a great way to learn what he needed to know.

"Okay, when did you get here?" Rouwa asked.

"To this city?" Jason squinted up at her again.

"Yes."

"This morning actually, like four or five hours ago. Let's see, when did your dad come home to live with you again?" he could tell they were uneasy without opening his eyes. "Well?"

He heard a quiet discussion going on above him, snippets of it floated down to him.

"I want to ask him…"

"I don't know…"

"He's working for Bartlett…"

"Mom wouldn't want us to."

The last argument won.

"We won't tell you," Raquel told him.

"I guess the game is over then." Jason sat up. "Thanks for letting me play."

"You're not sore?" Sammis asked incredulously.

"Mad? No, why should I be?"

"The other guys always get mad and yell."

"So there are people coming by trying to get you guys to talk?" Jason asked. "Your mom is smart to tell you not to talk to them." He got up and brushed the grass from his black cargo pants. "Do you know who those men are working for?"

"Some are from Bartlett, and we don't know who they are working for," Raquel told him. Jason could tell the boy desperately needed someone he could talk to about everything that was happening. "Who do you work for?"

"I pretty much work on my own," Jason answered. He thought of Benjamin but pushed the thought away. "Will your mom be back soon?"

Raquel shrugged, a glare from his sister had silenced him.

Out of the corner of his eye Jason saw Hannah teeter on the edge of the step for a second. He looked just in time to see her fall.

"Hannah!" Rouwa ran over to Hannah. "I told you to watch out for that step." She brushed furiously at her clothes then took the sobbing girl inside. Raquel wandered after them and Jason moved away from the house and sat on the bike rack to wait for Mrs. Black.

Sammis followed him and Jason helped him onto the bike rack.

"How come you want to talk to Mom so bad?" Sammis asked.

"Territ wouldn't tell me what happened to your dad." Jason told him. "If I know what happened I may find out who killed him."

"Someone shot my dad."

Jason nodded. That fit with Bartlett's story. "Do you know who it was?"

Sammis looked back toward the house to make sure his siblings were inside then leaned over confidentially. "Kora knows."

"Who's Kora?" Jason asked watching the cars go by.

"She's the oldest." Sammis' face looked too mature for his small body. "She knows what happened."

"How does she know?"

Sammis shrugged. "We aren't supposed to talk about it."

Jason nodded. "I understand."

They sat silently watching the neighbors returning from work.

"I like you," Sammis told him suddenly.

Jason looked down at him and smiled. "I like you, too. You're a good kid."

"Mom says we can't tell people about it 'cause there are people who want to hurt our family.'"

Jason nodded silently.

"Do you?"

Jason looked at the little eyes that hopefully searched his own. "No, Sammis. I'm not here to hurt your family. I want to help you. I want to catch the men responsible for killing your dad, so you won't have to be scared anymore."

"Good."

An old van pulled into the complex and Sammis jumped off the bike rack. "That's my mom."

Jason watched as the car moved slowly into a parking place. The moment the motor turned off Sammis raced across the parking lot to the driver's door and opened it for his mother. She was a well-built woman, not heavy but not overly slender. Her dark hair was pulled back from her face that plainly displayed the effect of the strain she had gone though over the last month. She gave Sammis a weary smile and hugged him against her. Jason could not hear what was said, but it was not long before Sammis pointed him out. She looked at him for a long moment, her eyes tired but determined. There was a warning in her look, but no hostility in her behavior. She opened the side door and pulled two grocery bags from the back seat and handed them to Sammis. Mrs. Black was soon joined by the other children who each took a load to the house.

Jason kept his distance, just watching the family interact. He could see she was weary from her trip and he did not want to put more stress on her. When they were finished she went inside without another glance at Jason. Sammis raced over to him.

"Mom says it's time for dinner. I got to go."

Jason smiled. "Take care of your mom, okay. She seems really tired."

Sammis nodded seriously. "I will."

"Good," Jason rose. "See you later."

FIVE

Jason took his time getting back to the hotel. The whole situation did not make sense. Taroe had been his contact with the last case and he had been very clear with the information he had given Jason. Bartlett was different. He did not even know what it was that was missing. Jason made a mental note to call Taroe and ask about Bartlett. He had a feeling this case was somehow related to the gang he had dealt with before. Regardless of the reasons, God had put him here to do something. He just needed to know what it was.

The sun was setting when he reached the hotel again. He opened the trunk, then stood there looking at the empty place where Benjamin's things had been. He sighed and pulled out his backpack.

"Why is this so hard?" he asked himself aloud. He had worked alone before but had grown accustomed to having someone to joke around with on the down hours, and to strategize with on missions. Joe Mckilligin, who had been Jason's spiritual mentor, had said something about having a friend in the area, but Jason was not ready to seek him out. He needed some time to sort out the events leading to Toby's death, and to Benjamin's sudden departure. He needed to figure out where he stood before bringing someone else into the mix.

"Sir?"

Jason let out his breath sharply. "Can't a guy get a moment

alone?" The irony struck him even as he said it.

"Just checking to make sure you're okay," the officer replied.

"I'm sorry." Jason ran his fingers through his hair, a habit he had developed on his first mission. "I've had a long day."

"This is hotel only parking here."

"Yes, sir." Jason gestured at the hotel. "I've got a room here. Have a good night."

The officer tipped his hat and walked across the street where he could keep an eye on him.

Jason closed the trunk and headed for the front door. A thin nervous man stood behind the counter. He chewed vigorously on a piece of gum as if to relieve his obvious tension.

"Can I help you?" he asked through his chewing.

"Yeah, I have a room reserved." Jason slid the paper across the desk.

"Roper, huh?" the man paused to chew. "You were pretty famous a while back, weren't you?"

Jason shrugged. "Yeah, I guess so."

"Can't remember why, but I never forget a name." He pecked away with one finger from each hand on the keyboard.

"That's good to know." Jason was relieved he did not remember. He was not in the mood to go through the whole 'are you really invincible?' discussion that usually arose.

"Your room number is 208." He looked up through his glasses at Jason. "It's on the second floor."

"Yeah, I kind of figured it was." Jason took the key and papers from him and turned to go.

"I have to say it," the man told him, still nervously chewing. "It's required because some people don't know and the boss doesn't want anyone feeling stupid. But I don't want anyone to think I think they're dumb you know. We had a shooting about a month ago just a few blocks from here. You never know what will make those people fly off the handle and blast you into eternity."

Jason grinned and turned back to the desk. This man could easily run his own comedy show. He had no idea what the shooting had to do with his room being on the second floor, but here was someone willing to talk about it. "Really?"

"You never know what guests are carrying guns now-a-days," he explained. "You know, I don't want to get shot over a room number. They say the guy they shot didn't even have a gun on him."

"Where was it?" Jason asked resting his arms on the high desk.

"I guess he'd left it at home or something."

Jason tried not to smile. "I mean, where was he shot?"

"Around one of the complexes, the ones closer to the lake."

"The lake is a pretty big attraction?"

"Oh definitely." He was straightening the papers on his desk and plunking the pens into the penholder. "It has a real name but no one knows what it is anymore."

"Not even you?"

He shook a pen at Jason. "Very funny. It was forgotten before I came here."

"Do you know who it was who was shot?"

"Sure, Toby Black." He stopped, straightening to attempt to return a bent paper clip to its original shape. "He was a nice guy."

"Did you know him?"

"Sure. Like I said, Toby was a nice guy. He was gone for a few months but came back a couple of weeks before he was killed." The clerk was still working at the clip.

"Why did he leave?" Jason asked.

"Hmm, I can't seem to get this straight."

"Let me try." Jason took the clip and switched it out with the one that had been on his paper. "There. Now why did he leave?"

"Wow, that was fast." He chewed nervously while he

examined the paper clip.

"Why did Toby leave?" Jason asked again. He was trying not to be pushy but this was his first real source of unbiased information.

"He worked some high paying job but the big men at the top just let him go one day. They didn't even give him a notice, and him with all those kids. The word is he got an offer from a guy in another city someplace…"

"No name?"

"Don't rub it in, it will come to me."

"Okay, we'll skip it for now." Jason sensed he was pumping the little man too much. "You really have an amazing memory to keep all this straight."

The man gave him a half smile. "I'll remember that city name sometime in the night."

"You can tell me tomorrow." Jason soothed. It was amazing what a little flattery could do. "So he went off and worked in some other city, then came back and got shot?"

"That's the way it was. Mike, that's the cop on this beat, said that it was his kids that found him first. Hold on, my gum's getting stale." He picked up the little trashcan and spit his gum into it. His hands shook a little as he unwrapped the next stick and popped it into his mouth. He chewed for a little while then returned to the counter. "Where were we?"

"You were telling me about the kids."

"Right, that's just how it happened. By the time the cops got there it was a done deal."

"I heard he was carrying something top secret. Any idea what it was?"

"Nah, everyone's pretty hush-hush about that." He popped in another stick of gum. "The story is, the kid who found him knows where it is, but I don't think they've gotten it out of him."

"Hmm. Well, thanks for the information."

"Sure. Thanks for fixing my clip." He held up the paper clip, still chewing furiously.

Jason smiled. "No problem."

"You'll have to take the stairs, the elevator is out of order," the clerk called after him.

"Thanks." Jason made his way up the stairs and let himself into the room. It was nice and spacious and seemed pretty clean. He tossed his backpack onto one of the beds and slumped on the overstuffed chair. His brain was numb and refused to connect the pieces of what he had heard. He would have to work on it in the morning before he went to see Bartlett.

Six

Benjamin silently slid the window open and slipped into the dark room. He moved stealthily to the bed and touched Territ gently.

Territ started, but Benjamin put a hand over his mouth. He waited until Territ relaxed, then released him. Putting a finger to his lips, Benjamin warned him not to speak. He pulled out a small notepad and handed it to Territ who sat up and squinted at it in the darkness.

Benjamin pulled out a flashlight, using the bed sheets to dim the light. He shone it onto the pad so that Territ could see it.

'*I am here to help you.*' was scrawled across the top of the page.

Benjamin handed Territ a pen.

'*Get lost,*' Territ wrote pushing harder than necessary.

Benjamin snatched the pen. '*Listen, I worked with your dad. He was involved in a gang in Frankford and he did a lot for me. I want to repay him by helping you.*' He offered the pen to Territ who hesitated, then took it.

'*How do I know you are not lying like the rest of them?*' Territ asked.

'*You'll have to take my word. I owe a lot to your dad.*' Benjamin returned the pad and pen.

'*Your word? I know who that Roper friend of yours is. My parents talked a lot about him, real hushed at night. He's the* one who messed up my dad's job in Frankford, sending my dad back here to get shot. For all I know he's the one behind it.' Territ shoved the pad at him accusingly.

'I'm not with Roper, I came on my own. I knew he would just get in the way.' Benjamin looked at Territ for a moment then added. 'I can get the formula through. No one would be watching me.'

Territ read what he had written and looked up, surprised. He opened his mouth but Benjamin quickly handed him the pen. Territ wrote 'How do you know it is a formula?' and handed over the notebook.

Benjamin shook his head at Territ before writing his reply. 'I told you, I worked very closely with your dad.'

'What was the formula for?' Territ asked handing the pad back with a conquering air.

Benjamin studied it a moment then scribbled 'I don't know.'

Territ looked at him as if weighing his options, then wrote with a steady hand. 'I'll think about it.'

Benjamin nodded and stuffed the notebook back into his pocket along with the pen and flashlight. He moved silently to the window and peered out before disappearing into the darkness.

Territ threw off the covers and went to the window.

The door behind him opened. "What do you think you're doing?" the night guard asked firmly.

"Stupid bed alarm," Territ grumbled. The guard crossed the room, shoved Territ aside, and pulled the window shut before radioing in the breach to security.

"Who opened this window?" the guard demanded.

"I did," Territ answered belligerently, crossing his arms on his chest.

"You know better than that. Get back in bed." The guard grabbed his arm and roughly guided him back to the bed. "Stay there. I'm not in the mood to deal with this tonight."

He waited until Territ was lying down before he left the room, leaving the door slightly ajar.

————

When Jason came down the next morning there was a different clerk at the desk.

"Good morning, sir," she said cheerily.

Jason ignored her, making a beeline for the door. He breathed deeply once he was out on the street, and headed for his car.

Fifteen minutes later he pulled up in front of the large drab building that served as Bartlett's headquarters. It was low and spread out over what Jason estimated to be about two acres of land. He was met at the door by a man in a suit who showed Jason inside. He watched Jason down the long hall to make sure he did not take any wrong turns.

Jason pushed open the door to Bartlett's office, startling Bartlett out of his chair.

"What do you want?" he demanded and then relaxed visibly. "Oh, it's you, Roper. I wasn't expecting you this early."

Jason's eyes fell on the big man who was sitting across the desk from Bartlett. The man rose slowly from his chair. Everything about him was big, not overweight, just large. His light blue eyes stood out in chilling contrast to his darkly tanned skin. Jason and the big man stood silently, sizing up one another.

Bartlett came around his desk to meet Jason. "Roper, this is Dothan, my maintenance man."

Jason nodded once and Dothan did not respond.

"That will be all, Dothan. Be sure you get those drains on the south side repaired."

The man gave a slight nod. His silence alone was terrifying. He gave Jason one last look, then left the room.

Bartlett gathered up the papers spread on his desk. "I

prefer you make an appointment before coming to see me. I'm very busy today." He put the papers into a filing cabinet, slid the drawer shut, and locked it. "Now, how can I help you?"

"I came to let you know I'll work on this case."

"I thought that was already decided." Bartlett gestured to the chair Dothan had occupied.

"It wasn't, but it is now." Jason didn't sit. "I'll see what I can find out from Territ."

"Good." Bartlett seated himself comfortably. "I'll have to ask you to leave our equipment in one piece."

"Yeah, I'm sorry about that."

"It was only a small investment down the drain." Bartlett replied with a hint of irritation in his voice. "I can work with you, if you will tell me what you need."

Jason nodded. "I'll remember that."

"It may be good that you came." Bartlett's tone softened. "Territ tried an escape last night and has been especially withdrawn today. Do you have time to talk to him?"

"Yeah, we might as well get to know each other."

———

Jason drove back toward the hotel as the midday sun beat down mercilessly. The rays reflected off the dash and into his eyes. Pulling his sunglasses out of a compartment, Jason slid them into place.

It helped with the glare but nothing else. Territ had been overly stoic. There had not even been a hint of a weakness in his guard. Jason had told him to play it up, but he was doing it a little too well. It was almost as if he had put up an extra wall when Jason had entered the room. Jason had spent nearly an hour trying to coax one response out of the boy but had gotten nothing at all.

Jason sighed and adjusted his glasses. He turned off on a side street and into a parking lot, pulling to a stop next to an old playground. A garland of orange netting decorated the dilapidated play equipment, showing it had been vandalized fairly recently. Jason got out and walked past it to the lake. There was a boat ramp, riddled with pot holes, for the people wealthy enough to own a boat. A new wooden dock stood parallel to the old one, its light colored wood standing out beautifully against the dark water.

There were a few children swimming in the shallows on the opposite side of the boat ramp. Their mothers sat on a bench up under the shade trees chatting about the latest town gossip.

He watched the children for a while as they splashed around in the water, wishing he could go back in time and be one of them. To live so secure, thinking everyone is just what they say they are, dreaming unreachable dreams into reality.

A movement to his right caught his eye and Jason moved his head slightly to make it out. It was a girl, tall and slender walking away from the lake. By the sweat on her brow Jason knew she had been walking for some time. Probably on some trail around the lake.

He watched her out of the corner of his eye. She carried herself just as her father had, erect and with refinement that did not fit her present class.

Kora glanced at him and he looked away, back at the children playing. He was not sure how to approach her. If what Sammis had said was true, she knew the secret they were all searching for. He would have to talk to her in a way that would not raise suspicions or put her in danger. Despite Bartlett's investigations, her father's killers were still at large.

Jason waited until she was out of sight before going back to his car. He shut the door and waited, unsure of his next move. He had no hard evidence for any of his suspicions, only the talk of the people who lived near the Blacks. He had checked with the agency that morning. Thomas Bartlett was working with them and was clear of suspicion as far as they were concerned. He put the car in gear and pulled out of the park. He could see the edge of the complex once he was on the street once more.

Benjamin stepped out onto the sidewalk and for an instant their eyes met. Jason slammed on the breaks as Benjamin ran past him in the opposite direction.

Jason put the car into reverse. The tires screeched on the pavement as he hit the gas. Benjamin turned off down a side street and disappeared into one of the buildings.

Jason pulled up to the curb and an officer knocked on the driver's window.

Jason rolled it down. "Yes?"

"There's no parking here." It was the same officer from the night before.

"What, were you just waiting here to tell me that?"

The officer folded his arms. "There's no parking here," he repeated stoically.

"Listen, this is an emergency," Jason told him. He could see it was a hopeless fight.

"Is it worth losing your car?"

Jason knew it was no use; he threw up his hands in frustration. Benjamin would be long gone before he could find a place to park. Sighing heavily, he put the car in gear once more, pulling slowly away from the forbidden curb.

He drove aimlessly down the streets. Why was Benjamin running from him? Had he returned that quickly to his former way of life?

He pulled to a stop and found himself in the complex parking lot. He looked up and there was little Sammis racing toward his car. The boy waited expectantly by the door watching Jason through the lightly tinted windows.

Jason pushed the door open.

"Hi, Mr. Roper." Sammis grinned at him. "I knew you

would come back."

Jason managed a weak smile.

"Nice car, is it yours?"

"Yep." Jason pulled the key out and pocketed it, automatically touching his cargo pocket to insure his Glock was in its place.

"Cool." Sammis ran his eyes over the car at a respectful distance. "Are you going to come up to our house again?" he finally asked. "Kora is home."

"I know." Jason pressed the lock button on the door as he got out, shutting the door behind him.

"You want to talk to her?" Sammis asked.

"No, not yet."

"Why?" Sammis' dark eyes were questioning.

Jason looked toward the apartment. Hannah was playing in the dirt by the steps with a brightly colored shovel and Rouwa was watching her from the top step between pages of her book.

Jason's eyes drifted down to the boy at his side. "Honestly, I don't know what to say to her."

"I just say 'Hi Kora,'" Sammis informed him innocently.

"Yes, well you are her brother. She doesn't know me." Jason looked up at the house once more. It seemed so quiet and peaceful.

"I wish you were her brother."

Jason looked down at him in surprise. "Why do you say that?"

"Cause then you would be my brother," Sammis answered kicking at some pebbles. "Do you like to play soccer?" he asked suddenly.

"Um, I guess so, I haven't played in a while." Jason ran his fingers through his hair. If only he could think of some way to broach the subject, to ask Kora what it was she knew without coming across as the bad guy.

Sammis grabbed his hand and pulled him toward the house. "I'll remind you."

Once he had gotten Jason moving, Sammis released his hand and ran ahead. He scrambled up the stairs, dodged Rouwa and disappeared into the house.

"How are you, Rouwa?" Jason asked.

She glanced up from her book. "Fine."

"Good." He hesitated, feeling awkward.

"My Mother doesn't wish to see you," She informed him without looking at him.

"I didn't come to see her."

That caught her attention and she closed the book, keeping her place with her finger. "Why did you come then?"

"I don't know," Jason told her honestly. "I guess I didn't really have anywhere else to go." He leaned on the stair rail. "I want you to know that I'm not trying to spy out your house or force your Mom to talk to me. When she's ready to talk I'll be around. I'm not going to push her into it before she's ready."

"So if she came out you wouldn't try to talk to her?" Rouwa asked skeptically.

"Well, I might say 'hi', but I'm not going to start throwing questions at her. I would really like to help, but I don't want to be pushy if my help isn't needed."

Rouwa looked at him for a long time, her mature eyes searching his for any sign of deceit. Without another word she rose and went inside.

Jason waited, watching Hannah digging around with her pink shovel.

"Mr. Roper, I can't find the ball." Sammis called from inside.

Jason heard Mrs. Black tell him not to yell and a moment later he appeared in the doorway. "I can't find it."

"What about Raquel? Does he know where it is?"

Sammis turned and disappeared once more into the house.

Jason wandered over to Hannah and crouched beside her dirt creation. "Whatcha building?"

"Dirt." She smiled up at him and returned to her digging.

"Are you making a castle?"

"No," She frowned in concentration as she pushed the shovel into the dirt. "I'm makin' dirt."

"The dirt is already there, God made the dirt."

"I'm makin' more." Hannah told him matter-of-factly.

"You might as well give it up."

Jason looked up to see Rouwa standing at the top of the stairs.

"She always makes dirt," Rouwa continued. "It's useless to tell her she's not."

Hannah paused her digging to look up at him as if to see if he believed her sister.

"God made the dirt," Jason told her under his breath. She giggled and returned to her digging.

Rouwa shifted uncomfortably as if she wished to say more. He stood and went to the stairs. "Was there something else?"

"I want to tell you that I appreciate what you said about giving Mom time. Even if you're one of Bartlett's men trying a new trick it was nice to hear."

"I meant it," Jason answered seriously, "You guys have been through a lot."

Sammis burst out of the door and almost knocked Rouwa off the stairs.

"Watch where you're going, Sammis," she told him firmly.

A partially inflated soccer ball rolled lazily down the steps, stopping on its own.

"Wow," Jason picked it up and it squished in his hand. "That's quite a ball."

"Is it too flat?" Sammis asked fearfully. Raquel appeared behind him looking hopeful.

Jason felt it and looked at their expectant faces. "Nah, we'll just have to kick harder."

Sammis beamed at him and scrambled down the stairs. Raquel followed at a slower pace in an attempt to keep his fourteen year old dignity.

"See you later, Rouwa." Jason called to her over his shoulder, following the boys away from the house.

"Okay," she responded, taking her seat on the steps once more.

"Thank you, Lord," Jason whispered smiling to himself. For the first time the defensive edge was gone from her voice. He was making headway.

SEVEN

Benjamin nodded to the door guard as he strode into the building. The guard nodded back, making no move to stop him. Benjamin smiled. Jason had not told Bartlett that they no longer worked together. This would make his job much easier. He dodged a burly man coming down the hall and continued confidently to Territ's room. He entered, not bothering to knock.

Territ looked up from his lunch, surprised by the invasion.

"Hi, Territ."

Territ returned to his lunch.

"Are we good?"

Territ looked up again, the confused look faded slowly. "Yeah, I guess so."

"Great. See, I know how much you like walking." Benjamin's face was serious. "So I got you this." He held out a woven bracelet.

Territ moved to take it but Benjamin pulled it away. "First we need an agreement."

The wall that went up was so obvious it was almost tangible.

"I'm going to ask Bartlett if you and I can go walking, to kind of get to know each other."

Territ tried to mask his interest.

"If you promise to keep this tracking device on, then you can go home or whatever for two hours or so each day. I'll have to negotiate some with the time but I think he'll agree since it was Roper's idea." Benjamin wiggled his fingers like quotation marks as he said the last two words.

Territ was unconvinced.

Benjamin pulled out a paper and scribbled on it then held it up. "Agree you dope, Roper has nothing to do with it."

Territ leaned back in his chair making it creak nicely. "I guess I could try it out for a day or two." He answered without enthusiasm.

Benjamin smiled and nodded his approval. The chair creaking was a nice touch.

"Okay, I'll go talk it over with Bartlett and see what he says."

"He'll say no," Territ told him, resuming his meal.

"Leave it to me."

———

Jason whaled the soccer ball sending it a full three feet down the makeshift field where Raquel easily retrieved it.

"It's too flat," he complained attempting to dribble it down the field.

Jason wiped the sweat from his eyes. "I agree. Mind if we take a break?"

"Nope." Sammis plopped down where he was and sprawled on the grass.

Jason and Raquel joined him.

"He's back again," Raquel said quietly, a hint of fear in his voice.

Jason looked at him. "Who?"

"Bartlett's man." Raquel was still speaking quietly as if he were afraid he would be overheard.

"Where?" Jason asked.

"Over by those trees, toward the lake."

Jason glanced up and for an instant fear fluttered in his heart. It was Dothan,. He stood gazing at them with steel blue eyes. "How often does he come?

Raquel shrugged. "He just comes. Mom said she talked to Bartlett about it but he says it is a security measure."

"Raquel, what do you know about your dad's death?"

Raquel's answer was what Jason had expected. "We're not supposed to talk about that."

———

Jason pushed open the front door of the hotel and was glad to see the nervous clerk was back on duty. "Hey, did you remember that name?" Jason asked good-naturedly.

"Frankford." The clerk answered with a grin. "I told you it would come to me. It hit me about two a.m. last night, but that's the way it usually goes."

"Frankford, huh? So they fired him from his good job there?" Jason thought out loud. He grinned at the clerk. "Thanks a lot."

"Anytime."

Jason started up the stairs then stopped. "You know my name but I never asked you yours."

"Bryan," the clerk answered popping another piece of gum into his mouth.

Jason went to his room and flopped down on his bed. Toby had told his family and the people of the town that he had gotten a high paying job in Frankford. In a way that was true if you count being a high ranking member of a gang as having a job. Jason frowned. Was the secret they were all after something he had taken from the gang before leaving? He let out a sigh and pushed himself off the bed. He smiled and brushed the bits of grass off the bedspread. The Lord had allowed him to slip comfortably into the lives of Toby's family. One by one he was gathering the clues he needed to sort out the mystery shrouding the death of Toby Black.

———

"I don't understand why Roper is not here discussing this," Bartlett told Benjamin. "After all I hired him, not you, for this job."

Benjamin sat across from him holding the tracking bracelet. "There is a lot to do on this case. We can't always be stuck together. There are some things I do for him."

Bartlett cocked his eyebrow. "While he plays soccer?"

"Um…"

"Or did you not know that was what he is doing?" Bartlett asked.

"Sure I knew." Benjamin leaned back comfortably in his chair. "The guy's got to blow steam somehow."

Bartlett frowned. "He is spending an awful lot of time chumming up to Black's family. I need him to get Territ to talk, not to make his family like him. Unless he knows something I don't." Bartlett's look was piercing

"He likes to get all the facts before he moves." Benjamin met his gaze without flinching. "That's the way he works."

Bartlett nodded, accepting the answer. "Get Roper to come and I'll think about it. Like I said, I hired him not you."

"He's going to be really ticked about this," Benjamin warned without moving.

"Let him be 'ticked' then. The records show that you were pretty heavily involved with the Jarris boys. I've got a lot at stake here."

Benjamin gave him a disgusted look. "I've got one little request and you are going to blow the whole thing over a status thing? You probably already know that I talked to Territ about it and he seemed to like the idea. If I can get him out and comfortable I can get him to talk."

"Give me the tracking device." Bartlett held out his hand. "I'll have my men look it over and get back with you."

"Don't bother, I'll just pick it up when I come by tomorrow."

"Roper sure lets you have a big part in this."

"I knew Toby better than he did, so we figured that would give the kid and I a little more in common." Benjamin responded coolly. It was all playing out just as he had planned.

EIGHT

Jason pulled up to the apartments just as Kora was leaving on her walk. He waited in the car, watching her until he was interrupted by a soft knock on the window. Sammis grinned at him and waved through the window. Jason looked back toward Kora but she was already out of sight. He pushed open the door.

"Hey, Sammis. What's up?"

"Are you going to come play?" Sammis asked.

Jason couldn't help smiling as he climbed out of the car. "Why do you think I'm here?"

"Kora just left," Sammis told him pointing in the direction she had gone. "She likes to walk around the lake, but it worries Mom when she's gone."

"I can understand why." Jason looked toward the lake once more.

"So do you want to play?" Sammis asked again.

"Is your mother home?" Jason asked walking toward the apartment.

"Yeah." Sammis seemed almost sad that she was.

"Okay, what shall we play?"

Sammis lit up once more.

"Play dirt," Hannah offered holding out her pink shovel full of dirt.

"No, Hannah, Mr. Roper doesn't want to play dirt," Sammis told her.

"Why not?" Jason asked. "I like playing dirt."

"You do?" Hannah laughed with the pleasure of the thought.

"Come on, Sammis, let's play dirt." Jason squatted next to Hannah. "What do I dig with?"

"I'll get you a shovel." Hannah ran up the steps and disappeared into the house.

"See if your mom will let you have an old cup." Jason called after her.

"Why do you want to play dirt?" Sammis kicked at the dirt distastefully.

"Because I'm going to build a castle with the works. A mote, a drawbridge, and a flag on the top," Jason told him.

Sammis squatted beside him. "You know how to do that?"

"Sure, don't you?"

Hannah reappeared with a broken blue shovel and a plastic cup. "Here you go!"

They were working on the second turret of the castle when Jason heard the apartment door open above him.

"Mr. Roper?"

Jason looked up to see Mrs. Black standing on the top step.

"Yes, Ma'am?" Jason stood and self-consciously brushed the dirt from his hands.

"I think it is time we talked, will you come in?"

Jason hesitated, trying hard to quell the excitement that welled inside him. He was sure that one talk with her would clear up so many of the questions that had been tangling themselves in his mind.

Mrs. Black smiled down at him. "Thank you for being sensitive, but I think we have waited long enough."

Jason climbed the stairs following her into the apartment. He shut the door and looked around. He was in the kitchen which was small but well kept. Hand drawn pictures graced the warn doors of the refrigerator, and there was a child's sandal on the floor under the edge of the counter. Jason took the straight backed chair she offered and sat with his back to the door.

"Would you like something to drink?"

"Um…" Jason hesitated. "Water would be great."

She got out a glass and set it on the counter. He glanced around the room, through a passageway behind the kitchen. He saw a couch and side table. Beside the hall there was a flight of stairs that led up to a second floor.

"What is it you need to know, Mr. Roper?" Mrs. Black asked pulling a pitcher of water from the refrigerator.

"Whatever you can tell me about Toby." Jason leaned forward. "If I could understand what it is he was doing, what he was carrying, I might be able to figure out who was behind what happened."

She nodded slowly as she watched the water flow into the glass. "There is a lot I won't be able to tell you at this time, and the rest you may already know."

"I'll take whatever I can," Jason told her reaching for the glass she offered. "Thank you."

She sat across from him and looked down at the scarred surface of the table. "Toby was working for an organization that must remain anonymous at this time. He worked for them for five years, going on several special assignments out of town and even out of state. The last assignment he was on was to Frankford to intercept the document that they killed him for."

"From the Jarris brothers?" Jason asked.

"Yes. Toby was working undercover, and was seen meeting with his contact by one of the gang members. Jarris himself was growing suspicious of Toby's motives when you showed up. You created enough distraction to keep the focus off of my husband. But you also stirred up enough trouble to delay the documents passing into other hands. The carrier got scared and skipped town, leaving Toby and the others who were after the document in a lurch. After several months Toby managed to track him to this area and get a hold of the document. From what I can tell, the killer intercepted the document when Toby was on the way to deliver it. He knew it would be dangerous. He said if he succeeded it would be worth his life to get the document out of their hands." She reached for a napkin in the holder on the table and wiped her eyes. "I think he knew he would die. When he left…" she dabbed her eyes again.

"You don't have to go on," Jason told her gently. He knew the story from there.

She shook her head. "Toby got the document and managed to hide it before they caught up with him. He was shot in the chest, which meant he was not running when they shot him." She dabbed her eyes again. "Knowing Toby he probably told them he no longer had the document but refused to tell them where he had hidden it. And they killed him."

She fell silent. Jason shifted uncomfortably and took a sip of his water, not daring to break the silence.

"I'm sorry." She wiped her eyes and smiled weakly through her grief. "There's not much more I can tell you about it with things where they are and my son being held in custody. I am praying you will be able to get to the bottom of this."

Jason realized the interview was over and rose to go.

"Mr. Roper."

Jason turned with his hand still on the door knob.

"Please remember there are children involved."

He nodded. "Yes, ma'am, I will."

———

"Hurry up, Territ," Benjamin hissed.

Territ scrambled behind the dumpster and crouched beside him. "What are we doing?"

"We're getting the formula."

"What?"

"Keep it down," Benjamin warned. "This is our only chance to get away."

"Bartlett said if I run he'll take my whole family apart," Territ reminded him fiercely.

"We won't be gone long enough for him to notice," Benjamin assured him. "Now where is it? I've got buyers who are waiting for it across the state lines." Benjamin moved through the shadows with Territ on his heels.

"That would serve him right if we sold it," Territ whispered moodily. "Bartlett killed my dad, he's not getting the formula too."

Benjamin stopped to look at Territ "Bartlett killed him?" he asked in surprise.

"Yeah, the back stabbing..."

Benjamin cut him off "How do you know? I thought you didn't get there until after he was shot."

"I didn't, but Kora was there when it happened."

"Your sister?" Benjamin asked. "Why didn't you tell me?"

Territ closed up. "I don't have to tell you anything."

"Yeah, well, you could at least have told me that," Benjamin retorted. "Here I got you out so we could get that formula out of Bartlett's reach and you were just leading me on. How am I supposed to help you if you're holding out on me?"

Territ just looked at him sullenly.

Absorbed in his thoughts Benjamin stared back at the apartments. He had to get to Kora before Bartlett did.

NINE

The Blacks were just sitting down to dinner when the door burst open.

"Nobody move." A man brandishing a handgun planted himself by the door keeping the family covered. Kora rose from the table fearfully and her eyes met her mother's. The man covered them as two others entered the room. All three wore dark clothes and sunglasses that hid their eyes.

"You." They gestured at Kora. "Come with us."

"No," she whispered in terror.

He turned the gun on her. "We don't have a lot of time, Missy. You got two minutes max to grab your things."

Kora looked at her mother for help and she rose. "What is the meaning of this? You can't just...?"

The man ignored her. "Your time's ticking, Kora. We're trying to be nice." The man's voice was strained with urgency. He showed Mrs. Black something Kora could not see. She met his eyes and then turned to Kora.

"Go get your things," Mrs. Black told her gently.

Kora looked confused. Tears streaked her face. "But Mom..."

"Kora, it's just like Territ. There's nothing we can do. I don't want you to get hurt." Silent tears ran down Mrs. Black's careworn face as she pushed her daughter toward the stairs.

One of the men moved to follow her, but Raquel stood in his way. The man shoved him aside and climbed the stairs to Kora's room with Raquel right behind him. She was shoving things into a small duffle bag on her bed when they entered the room.

"Let's go."

She hesitated and he took her arm, guiding her down the steps.

"Don't touch her," Raquel yelled, flying at him.

He was met by the barrel of the man's gun. "Stay out of this, boy, or someone will get hurt."

Raquel looked past him at his sister, tears welling up in his eyes.

Kora attempted to smile through her tears. "Take care of Mom for me."

He nodded, the tears spilling over onto his hot cheeks as the man guided her down the stairs. They watched helplessly as the men took her away. The first man covered them until they had loaded her into the waiting van then hurried to join them.

The van sped down the street and soon disappeared from sight.

"I hate those men," Raquel spat angrily.

"Raquel." Mrs. Black's tone held a warning but she said no more. What more could she tell him? She had nothing to comfort him with, no reassurances to give him. She looked up at the darkening sky. "Protect her, Lord," she whispered hugging her remaining children close.

———

Jason woke suddenly; the room was dark and silent. He sat up slowly and rubbed his face with his hands. He sat for a moment with his face in his hands, strangely aware that he was not alone.

"What do you want?" His voice sounded loud in the stillness.

"I need your help." It was a woman's voice, tired and with a twinge of fear.

Roper looked up but could only make out her outline against the door. "Who are you?"

"It's better if you do not know," she answered quietly. "If they knew I came…" She let her words drift into silence.

Roper waited and soon she spoke again. "It is my niece. They have taken her…," she began hesitantly, but as she spoke her voice gained an edge of urgency. "My brother was killed a few months ago and took with him the location of a formula someone else wanted very badly. When the men, they are from a branch of the FBI, found my brother he had just died and my nephew was kneeling over him. I don't know how much you already know. My sister-in-law, Chandra, said I was to come to you."

"So much for me not knowing who you are," Jason mumbled, throwing the covers off and placing his bare feet on the floor. He rested his elbows on the knees of his cargo pants and supported his chin with his palm, waiting for her to continue.

"Bartlett has been holding my nephew for some time, trying to protect him from those who would steal the secret. A few days ago Bartlett started letting Territ, that's my nephew, go home for about two hours a day."

"That's news to me," Jason interrupted. "When did that start?" He did nothing to conceal his irritation. He had been out the last few days asking the locals what they knew about Toby's shooting. Why would Bartlett take such a big step without letting him know?

"I just told you, about two days ago," the lady paused. "Maybe I came to the wrong person."

"No, I'm sorry." Jason sighed. "Go on with your story."

She hesitated as if deciding and then went on. "Somehow, they lost track of him for about an hour yesterday. When he turned up they discovered that it is my niece, Toby's eldest, who actually has the location of the secret formula. They went at once to the house but were too late. If this formula gets into the wrong hands terrible things will happen." Again she fell silent.

"What kind of formula is it?" Jason asked.

"I don't really know, something that can be used to create an unstoppable weapon." She put a thin hand to her forehead. "I didn't understand the bits and pieces I heard."

"What were they too late for?" Jason asked to return her attention to her story.

"Earlier tonight, just hours before Bartlett's men arrived, some men came with guns to my brother's house and simply took her away. There was nothing the family could do to stop them."

"What exactly do you want me to do?"

She wrung her hands in agony. "I don't know what we can do. Chandra just told me to come to you. She said you could be trusted."

"So Bartlett's men have her?"

"No." She seemed surprised that he would ask. "Bartlett is trying to help them. He is working with the FBI to secure the formula before it gets into the wrong hands."

"Then where is she?"

"There is a house several miles out of town where we believe she has been taken. Chandra thinks it is the people Toby was mixed up with, the ones who paid him to steal the formula from the FBI agent. The kidnappers must have found out she knows where the formula is because they have taken every precaution to secure her. They are a part of a big racket and have more than enough money to guard her well. With all the guards and things, Chandra is afraid no one would be able to get to her." The woman was wringing her hands again.

"The Blacks do not like Bartlett and his men," Jason told her bluntly.

"Yes, that is what their mother has coached them to say. You know how kids are. They trust whoever comes along and tell them everything they know. In order to protect her children Mrs. Black has made them think that it is Bartlett's men who are the enemies because she has no way of telling Bartlett's men from men from this other group."

"Okay." Jason stood and ran his hand through his damp hair. "So you want me to go get her?"

"Yes, if there is any possibility of saving her." Her voice was pleading. "You are the only one who could go in. Even if the guards saw you they couldn't stop you."

"How do I know you are telling the truth?" Jason asked her as he walked the length of the room.

"Why else would I be here?"

"You are saying all this time Bartlett has been trying to protect the formula while Territ, coached to think Bartlett is bad, is holding out?"

"Territ is a stubborn boy. He thought by not telling he would be protecting his sister."

"I need more proof to go on." Jason spoke more to himself than to her.

"Go and talk to the family if you must, but Chandra is pretty shook up. Bartlett would know more about it."

"That's understandable."

She stepped aside as Jason reached past her to open the door. He took her arm and gently guided her out into the hall. She was thin and had dark hair, but other than that there was no physical resemblance to Toby.

"There is something else you need to know," she told him urgently, glancing around to insure the hall was empty.

"What's that?" Jason had had enough of their meeting.

"They sent a message saying that if she leaves the secure

house they will attack her family as they did her father."

Jason nodded and closed the door behind her. He leaned against it and listened for the stair door to close before leaving his position. Slipping down the hall he opened the door quietly. He heard the door to the lobby close with an ominous boom that echoed in the empty stairwell. He returned to his room and hurriedly pulled on his shoes.

His quick footsteps echoed in the stairwell as he made his way to the lobby. Bryan was bending over something at the front desk when Jason passed.

"The manager doesn't approve of late night visitors," Bryan told him through his gum.

"Neither do I," Jason answered, peering out the glass front door. She was nowhere in sight. He turned to Bryan. "Who was she?"

"How should I know? She came to visit you," Bryan replied absently.

"How exactly did she get into my room?" Jason asked accusingly. "Is it normal for the night clerk to hand out keys?"

"She said she knew you," Bryan answered defensively.

"Then she would have knocked like anyone else." Jason shot back. "Why did you give her a key to my room?"

"Hey, you're supposed to be invincible. What could she do to you?"

Jason raked both hands through his hair. "I'm going to have you fired," he told Bryan bluntly. "I have just as much right to privacy as any of the other guests. You think being invincible somehow makes me lower than everyone else, like some sort of rug to walk over?" Jason demanded.

"Mr. Roper."

"Oh, don't give me that," Jason interrupted. "You gave a key to the room I am paying for to someone you don't even know."

"She was in trouble," Bryan answered mater-of-factly.

"You're supposed to be some sort of hero. Besides, you're not paying for the room. That bigwig guy is."

"Money's money. Why does it matter who it is coming from? The room is being paid for and it's for my use."

Bryan took some papers to his file drawer. "I thought you were interested in the Black's case, so I let her in."

Jason struggled to calm himself. This wasn't how a Christian was supposed to act. He knew that, but sometimes he did not feel like a Christian. He wondered how Mckilligin was able to be a cop and still manage to live like Jesus told His followers to live. Jason took a deep breath and let it out forcefully. "Does she still have the key?"

"Don't be daft. I didn't let her keep it."

"Thank you." Jason's calmness was forced.

Leaving Bryan to his chewing, Jason returned to his room and packed his things.

"Here we go again," he muttered, swinging his backpack onto his shoulder.

T_{EN}

"Bartlett, I have to be honest with you, you fit nicely into the mold of the bad guy in this situation." Jason leaned forward, his eyes locking with Bartlett's. "Everyone I've talked to, and everything I've learned so far, could be describing you instead of this unnamed racketeer. You are not real popular in this town."

"I can see how you might think that with the information you have been given." Bartlett rose and unlocked a file drawer. "The people here are not overly fond of the authorities, police and such, because of family ties, or their own unlawful activities. I think it is time I let you in on a little more of what is going on."

Jason waited as the big man located the thick file and pulled it out.

"This will help you understand."

Jason pulled his chair up to the desk as Bartlett laid out the papers before him. "What is all this?"

"As you know Toby was a member of the Jarris brother's gang that you busted up in Frankford."

Jason nodded.

"You took care of that branch of the operation but that was only a small part of what was actually going on." Bartlett passed him a paper that bore the official seal of the FBI. "The Boss, I cannot disclose his name at this time due to security reasons, was playing that racket as what you might think of as a side show, while the real business was going on undercover. Information being passed and things like that. I wouldn't be surprised if even your colleague knew nothing about it despite his close workings with the late Toby Black. What we are after is what they were processing when you broke up the gang. My men and I have been following their actions for years now, and we believe Toby followed the information here. He did not run away from Frankford, he was following the man carrying the formula. We believe he meant to pass it on to the next man up, and that he got the document just before he was killed."

Jason nodded slowly, drinking in the information on the papers before him. This story coincided perfectly with what he had learned from Mrs. Black. Mrs. Black said Toby had thought it was worth his life to get that formula out of someone's reach. If only he knew who Toby was trying to get the document to, and who he was trying to keep it from.

"But Toby didn't have the document on him when you found him?" Jason asked glancing up from the papers.

"That's right."

"How do you know his killer doesn't have it?" Jason picked up another set of papers and began flipping through it.

"We have our sources. Surely the kidnapping proves they are still searching for it."

Jason nodded, scanning the papers he held.

"It has been necessary to assume a more behind-the-scenes position here due to the sensitivity of the situation at hand. I must admit I have come across as the bad guy in more than one occasion but there are those who would not be as lenient as I have been with Territ. We have had to keep him here for his own safety. If the Boss' men got a hold of him they would do anything to get their hands on that formula. Do you understand the delicacy of the situation?"

"I think so." Jason lowered the papers to his lap.

"We are trying to draw out the Boss and his men without getting a lot of agents involved, which is why you were called in. Taroe hoped that you would be able to get Territ to talk and get the location without endangering the family. Now Kora is the one we need to protect but she is already out of our hands."

Jason handed the stack of papers back to Bartlett. "Why didn't you tell me this when I got here?"

Bartlett smiled a little. "It's my turn to be honest." He gathered up the papers and went to return the file to its place. "I didn't trust you. Taroe has worked with you before and knows you. I hadn't. I didn't want to blow all we have worked for on some teenage hero."

Jason understood. He was almost twenty, but compared to Bartlett he had very little experience in the field. "Why isn't Mr. Taroe on this case?"

"Taroe is involved in another case. Besides, he doesn't have the background I do on this one."

"I see."

"Are you still willing to help?"

Jason thought for a moment, then nodded. "I'll need a layout of the place with a detailed list of the security features of the house, a geographical map of the surrounding area, and a box of forty caliber bullets."

"We don't want any shooting," Bartlett cautioned. "We need her alive."

"You get me what I asked for and I'll get her for you." Jason rose and held out his hand to Bartlett who shook it firmly.

"I'll get you a description of the girl as well."

"The description isn't necessary. I've seen her a couple of times."

"Thank you, Roper. You are doing your country a great service."

Jason nodded once in response. "I may need some other

supplies depending on what security they have up."

Bartlett nodded, "I'll get my men on it."

———

"You're late again," Grant told Benjamin with triumph in his voice.

Benjamin ignored him. He slid his time card and stuffed it back into his pocket.

"That's the second time this week," Grant reminded him.

"I had a rough night," Benjamin told him, absently pinning on his badge.

"Nightmares?" Grant asked with feigned concern. "I hear criminals usually struggle with that."

"Yeah. They were all about you," Benjamin muttered brushing past him. He went to the basement and grabbed a vacuum. Returning to the first floor, Benjamin walked down the long office lined hallway and plugged it in. Leaving the vacuum he poked his head into the first office. "I'm going to vacuum. Do you want me to close your door?"

The man behind the desk nodded and went back to his phone call. Benjamin pulled the door closed and went to the second office.

"You're late again."

Benjamin nodded. "I know, I'm sorry."

"I hired you to keep this place clean."

"Yes sir." Inside Benjamin chafed against the man's condescending tone. Here he was playing janitor to some rich over-weight guy when he could easily take everything the man had and probably never get caught.

"With your record I took a chance when I hired you." The man continued. "Don't abuse my generosity."

Benjamin looked down, trying to look ashamed. His eyes fell on a blank check lying on the desk. How easy it would be.

The man followed Benjamin's gaze to the check. He

slapped a fat hand onto the check and slid it into his drawer.

Benjamin did not attempt to hide his amusement.

"What are you smirking about?" the man asked, eyeing Benjamin.

"Nothing. Do you want your door closed when I vacuum?"

"No, not this time." The man's tone was suspicious.

Benjamin left the office and shut the doors of the ones who he knew preferred it. He grabbed the vacuum and set to work. He would be free of this once he got his hands on that formula.

———

"Benjamin?"

Benjamin didn't look up from the window he was washing. "Yeah."

"What are you doing here?"

"What does it look like I'm doing, Roper? I'm washing windows," Benjamin replied coolly.

Jason hesitated. Benjamin obviously did not want to talk. "How's it going? I haven't seen you in a while."

"Fine." Benjamin gave the window one last swipe with a paper towel and moved on to the next window.

"Bartlett told me you were still coming around to see Territ."

Benjamin shrugged. "I guess I like the kid."

"You're the one who suggested Bartlett let him get out more."

"You're just full of great observations," Benjamin answered. The squeegee squeaked across the wet pane.

"Why were you running from me the other day?" Jason finally asked. "And why were you pretending you are still working with me?"

Benjamin shrugged. "Connections are there to be used."

"So you were playing along all this time just to get here?"

Jason was trying hard to stay calm. "To wash windows?"

"Some of us have to work for a living," Benjamin told him, wiping a bead of sweat from his forehead with the back of his hand.

"Yeah, well some people can't get jobs," Jason retorted. "You knew we would be sent here. You knew Toby was following the formula and you were just biding your time."

Benjamin didn't answer.

"Were you supposed to meet him here. Was that how you planned it? But then he got killed and you were left with nothing."

"I'll find it," Benjamin muttered.

"So you're working with the men who took her?"

Benjamin looked at him then caught himself and went back to the window but not before Jason saw the surprise in his face.

"Don't mess with the girl," Benjamin warned. "She's where she needs to be. You don't understand what is happening."

"I would if you would fill me in," Jason answered angrily. "I'm just trying to do my job. What are you trying to do?"

"Get these windows cleaned before lunch," Benjamin answered.

Jason shook his head. "I thought...it doesn't matter. Have fun with your windows."

"Roper."

Jason turned and waited.

"Leave the girl alone."

Jason looked at him for a long moment, then turned and walked away without looking back. He had been on his own before, and he could do it again. He was beginning to think his father was right. Trust was a sign of weakness. Those who trusted always got hurt.

ELEVEN

Jason slid under the sensor and crept toward the house. He dropped to the ground as a guard rounded the corner of the house. For kidnappers they certainly were taking their job seriously. When the man was gone Jason scrambled to his feet and ran silently to the back window. He pulled out a little tool kit and selected the glass cutter. Deftly scoring a piece big enough for his arm to fit through, he fastened a small suction cup to the piece. Holding the suction cup steady with one hand he gave the glass a sharp tap to break it loose and pulled it from the window. Jason ducked beneath the window, waiting. Nothing moved inside. Jason rose, reached through the hole he had made, and carefully deactivated the alarm.

Creeping slowly to the edge of the house, Jason peered around the corner. There was no one in sight, but it would not be long before the guard passed again. Jason pulled out his gun and waited. The minutes stretched on as he crouched there. Finally he heard the guard approaching. He flattened himself against the wall of the house and waited. The guard appeared and Jason struck him with the butt of his gun. The guard crumpled without a sound. Dragging him around the corner, he rolled the guard up against the side of the house where he would be less noticeable. Jason took a moment to check his work. The cameras were frozen, and the guard was out of the way. He nodded and went back to the window. Carefully reaching through, he slid the window lock. Nothing. Jason grinned. Bartlett had been thorough in the security description.

Glancing around, he silently pushed the window up and climbed in. He had five minutes to get Kora and get out. He glanced around the room, the light had not yet faded from the sky outside and the dusky light that came in the window made it easy to make out the furniture in the room. He moved to the bedside, pulling out his gun. It wasn't loaded because he had no reason to use it, but he needed the persuasive power it offered.

The bed was empty. Jason's eyes narrowed. If Bartlett was lying to get him out of the way… Something connected with the back of his head, throwing him off balance.

He spun to find Kora looking up at him with big scared eyes. She was wearing brightly colored pajama pants and a loose t-shirt.

"Don't make any noise," Jason warned, turning the gun on her. He could tell she was trying to remember where she had seen him before.

Jason scanned the room, his eyes coming to rest on the closet. Keeping her covered with the unloaded gun he went and opened it. Reaching through the clothes, Jason pushed on the walls to make sure they were firm.

"Okay, get your clothes. I recommend something comfortable. You have two minutes to change." Jason shoved aside the few hanging clothes to give her more room and stepped out of her way.

She stared at him in shock. "What are you trying to do?"

"I'm rescuing you," Jason told her. "Hurry up, once two minutes are up you'll be stuck in your PJs."

"I don't need to be rescued. I'm not in trouble," she informed him.

"Yeah, I know. You keep saying that and we'll tell them

I kidnapped you," Jason told her. "Get your stuff."

She saw he meant it and grabbed her things. He grabbed her arm as she passed.

"Don't try to knock on the wall or alert anyone, I'll be waiting."

She nodded silently and hurried to change.

Jason waited, glancing at his watch to make sure she didn't take longer than he had said. He went to the clock on the nightstand and turned off the alarm. He did not think they would make it out without detection, but if they did he wanted to have as much get-away time as possible.

She emerged wearing jeans and a different t-shirt. "You're making a huge mistake. I'm not…"

"Shh." Jason tossed her the tennis shoes he had found. "They told me all about it. You are afraid to leave because they'll hurt your family. I'll get you out and there's someone who promises to keep you out of their hands."

"They?" she asked pulling on her shoes. "What are you talking about? I'm in a safe house now."

Jason nodded. "Sure, if that's the way you cope with it, that's fine. Let's go."

She rose. "Who are you working for?"

"We don't have time to talk it all out," Jason informed her peering out the window.

"I think we need to," she responded firmly. "I'm not coming with you."

Jason turned to see her sitting on the bed again. "Listen, Kora, I know about your situation. I read just about the whole file. You need to get out of this, and I'm going to help you whether you like it or not. Get up."

She rose once more, wearing a concerned frown. "He's hired you to kidnap me. You're that invincible guy. Bartlett got you to do his dirty work." She grabbed a pen from the nightstand and ran to the dresser and began scratching vigorously on its surface.

Jason sprinted across the room and grabbed the pen out of her hand, shoving her away from the dresser. He glanced at the large crudely made letters cut into the polished surface of the wood. R O P E R. The e was missing the middle line and the last R wasn't complete but the word was plain.

"Why did you have to do that?" Jason demanded in a harsh whisper.

"I want them to know who the crook is," She responded, her eyes burning with anger. "People think you are a hero, you tricked my family into thinking you're a hero."

"I'm helping you," Jason reminded her as he steered her toward the open window. "Now keep quiet."

She pulled back a little at the window. "Please, let me stay. You don't know what you're doing."

"They told me you would beg, but this is ridiculous. Listen, nothing is going to happen to your family. Once you are out of here you won't have to be afraid," Jason reassured her. "Okay, I'm going to open this window and we are going to get out and go straight across the yard and keep going. You got it?"

"Please don't take me," she begged, the fire gone from her eyes.

Jason shook his head. "At this point I'm already committed." He looked out to make sure no one was coming and something moved behind him.

Jason spun just in time to see Kora racing for the door. He leapt after her, grabbing her by the ankles and knocking her to the ground. She struggled as he pulled her toward the window and shoved her through. He had expected some resistance but this was more than he had anticipated. He jumped through and grabbed her again as she made a bee line for the front of the house. Holding tightly to her forearm Jason pressed the gun to her ribs.

"Don't move."

She obeyed and Jason could feel her trembling.

"Bartlett hired you, didn't he?" she asked fearfully. "You're one of his men."

"No, I'm not 'one of his men.'" Jason pulled her across the well-trimmed lawn.

"You're working for him though," She pressed. "Please don't take me to him. He's working for terrible men and… please don't take me."

Jason pulled her down and they crawled together under the sensor.

"You don't know what you're doing. You're working for the wrong people," she told him once they were on the other side. "I'm doing this for your good."

"What's for my good?" Jason was exasperated.

"This." She stuck her hand into the sensor. A loud alarm shattered the stillness of the night and immediately the house came alive.

Jason smacked his palm to his forehead. They had been so close.

It was amazing how fast they were spotted. Gunfire broke out behind them, almost drowned out by the wailing alarm. The marksmanship of her captors was impressive. Not one of the bullets touched Kora, while Jason felt as if he were in the midst of a small hail storm. He grabbed Kora's arm and pushed her ahead, trying to keep himself in a position to shield her. He propelled her through the thin stand of trees towards the hole in the fence. The gunfire faded as quickly as it had started. They knew who he was and that he could not be stopped. A single bullet hit the tree just ahead of him with a dull thump throwing bark and tiny splinters into the air. Its message was clear to Jason, and he knew they would not give up until they had the girl again.

As they ran the few yards to his car, Kora stumbled and

fell hard striking her head on one of the many roots that were woven through the path. Jason grabbed her arm. She did not respond.

"What are the chances?" Jason groaned glancing behind him. He could hear the voices of the guards shouting commands somewhere behind them. He scooped her up, and covered the remaining distance in a few, quick steps. He fumbled with the handle of the driver's door. Using his knee on the driver's seat to keep his balance he awkwardly maneuvered her limp body into the passenger's seat. He slid into his seat and jammed the key into the ignition. The tires spun in the loose dirt kicking up a cloud behind them as they took off down the dusty road.

———

"Hey, Benjamin, I just got a scoop on that hero of yours." Grant called across the musty basement. "He was all over the news."

"Yeah?" Benjamin showed no enthusiasm over the news. Grant was constantly trying to pick a fight, but at the present Benjamin needed the job more than the taste of revenge. "Being a lowly janitor I guess you wouldn't have seen the news," Grant observed loftily.

"Nope. Some of us actually work for a living." Benjamin heaved the mop bucket up to the sink and poured out the dirty water. He was not in the mood for this. Cleanup had taken longer than normal tonight thanks to some secretary spilling a whole pot of coffee on the break room floor.

"You won't be such a big fan once you hear what he did," Grant taunted.

"At least he has fans," Benjamin muttered. He grabbed the hose and sprayed out the bucket.

"He's a kidnapper." Grant's smile disappeared as Benjamin turned on him.

"Who did he kidnap?" Benjamin's intensity threw Grant off guard.

"I thought you weren't…"

Benjamin slammed Grant against the wall, his thumbs pressing on Grant's windpipe. "Who was it?"

"I'll have you fired." Grant hissed trying hard to breath.

Benjamin's eyes narrowed. "Do you think I really care?"

Someone opened the door behind them. Benjamin dropped Grant to the floor and turned to face the newcomer. "Myron, who did Roper kidnap?"

Myron was startled by the question. He looked at the bucket that had fallen from the sink and then at Grant on the floor. "Some girl," he said with a shrug. "It was some sort of special news bulletin. Apparently it happened earlier tonight, around ten I guess, and they really want her back. They have an all-points bulletin out. I don't remember her name," he finished absently.

Grant scrambled to his feet, rubbing his throat. "You'll be sorry." He spat at Benjamin, who was skillfully ignoring him.

Benjamin's eyes locked with the older man's. "Was her name Kora?"

Myron looked surprised. "Yeah, that's right. I remember now, it was Kora Black."

"Oh, no," Benjamin breathed. He ran for the door and burst through, plowing into Grant's office mate who was waiting to lock up. Benjamin shoved him aside. He raced through the empty offices and out into the street. He turned toward the setting sun and ran as if his life depended on it. He was pretty sure someone else's did.

TWELVE

Jason knew there was something wrong as soon as he opened his car door. Bartlett was there as promised but he wasn't alone. Jason glanced at Kora. She had come to and was looking past Jason at the men waiting. There was pure fear in her eyes. A cold sick feeling washed over him, suddenly it was all too clear. He had bought into Bartlett's plan and kidnapped an innocent, placing her in terrible danger. Jason grabbed the handle but the door didn't close, he looked up to see Dothan's huge form above him. His eyes met Dothan's cold blue eyes and a wave of fear washed over him, tightening the knot in his stomach.

"Get out," Bartlett ordered. There was a tinge of pleasure in his commanding tone.

Jason grabbed the key to start the car. Something struck him hard, slamming his head against the headrest. The man's muscular arm held him firmly against the seat and Jason felt the key being wrenched from his hand with strength he could not withstand. The man released him and Jason knew there was nothing he could do. He had made the worst mistake of his life, and now he had to face the consequences. He plowed his fingertips into his hair, pressing his forehead against his palms. Another man pulled on the handle of the passenger door and Kora gave a little cry of fear. Her hand flew to the lock.

"Lord, I'm so sorry," Jason whispered, his soul in aguish.

"I didn't know."

Dothan grabbed Jason's arm and wrenched him from the car. Jason felt no pain as he was slammed against the side of his car. Dothan held him as another man frisked him and took his gun. Dothan pulled Jason off the car and delivered him to two other broad-shouldered men who had emerged from the waiting van. Jason watched helplessly as the other man went for Kora.

Tears streaked Kora's face as she struggled to keep him out. They were toying with her, pressing unlock and pulling on the handle giving her just enough time to lock it again.

Without warning the man by her door smashed his gloved hand through the passenger window. Kora screamed and scrambled to get away from them. In moments the door was opened and she too was jerked from the car.

Jason struggled against the men who held him. "Let her go, Bartlett. Please."

Bartlett laughed cruelly. "Don't be ridiculous, Roper. You're the one who brought her to us. Besides, I have the feeling that you didn't pay any mind to her begging."

"I didn't know," Jason bit his lip, fighting hard against the emotions that flooded over him. "You lied to me, Bartlett. Please, I didn't know. Just let her go."

"Yes, I lied, and obviously did it very well, but it was your choice to go and get her for me." Bartlett shook his head. "It sickens me to see a big tough guy like yourself blubbering like a baby. Besides, I've got something planned for you too."

"Do it to me, whatever you had against this girl, I'll pay for it," Jason begged.

"No," Bartlett was serious again. "If it were a matter of money, I might take you up on it, double or triple the sum and let you cover it. This is something else, something only Kora can help me with. Isn't that right?"

Kora, like Jason, was being held between two burly men.

She was trembling hard, and tears were still running down her face but she kept her head down and refused to respond.

"I guess you don't mind if we get rid of your kidnapper." Bartlett motioned to the men and they pushed her toward the dark water of the lake. "See, we knew how you would feel, so we planned a little vacation for him, and we'll give you the pleasure of a front row seat at the show. You see, Hero Boy here is invincible, and he enjoys popping up where he's not wanted. But we have some friends who would like to see him, shall we say, out of the picture." He turned to Jason. "After this terrible kidnapping you've committed no one will care if you simply disappear for a very long time."

"Let her go," Jason begged weakly. "I'll cooperate, just let her go."

"Touching," Bartlett replied sarcastically. "But you don't have a choice."

Jason dropped hard pulling the men off balance and managing to free one of his arms. He swung at his remaining captor, planting his fist under the man's square jaw, which sent the surprised man reeling backwards in pain, clutching his face.

"Are you sure you want to keep going?" By the calmness in Bartlett's voice Jason knew what he would see before he turned to look. Bartlett had moved to Kora's side and was pointing his gun at her thigh. "We need her alive, but a little damage won't hurt our purpose any," Bartlett told him.

Jason sighed hard, seeming to wilt a little as he did. Silent tears of sorrow and defeat spilled over and slid down his cheeks as he bowed his head to hide them.

The men grabbed his arms once more, muttering threats and using more force than was necessary to hold him.

"That was a lovely exhibition, Roper but we don't have time for any more." Bartlett handed the gun to one of his men. "If you try anything else he'll shoot her. Is that clear?"

Jason didn't respond. Defeated, he cried out inside for a chance to make it right.

"Good. Get him ready."

Jason didn't resist as his hands were cuffed behind him. His captors, still sore from his previous escape, shoved him roughly to the ground but Jason felt no pain. His ankles were pulled up behind him and cuffed to a length of chain attached to his wrists.

"Dothan, what's taking so long?" Bartlett demanded.

Jason watched as the big man approached carrying a large object, his muscles bulging with the effort. He paused, waiting for Bartlett's instruction.

"Go ahead and take it to the dock. Hero cost us a bit more time with his petty antics so we don't have time to take him all the way out."

———

Benjamin saw Roper's mustang up ahead in the parking lot of The Lake and ducked off the main road onto a little dirt path. He sprinted through the little wooded area that surrounded the park, slowing as he neared the lot. He could make out a group of men up ahead in the dim light of the street lamps. They were clumped together around something on the ground. Benjamin scanned the men, and spotted the girl who was held firmly between two men. He felt for his gun and let out an exasperated sigh. He had been banned from carrying it at work because of the trouble with Grant. There was nothing Benjamin could do against so many. All he could do was bide his time and be ready when his chance came.

———

"Won't they find him if he's close to shore?" one of the men holding Kora asked skeptically.

"We can't take the chance of losing our little prize." Bartlett smiled with amusement at the horror stricken look on Kora's face. "Besides, who will be looking here? I can send someone out after this blows over to move him further out."

She watched as they lifted her kidnapper from the ground and carried him toward the murky water. Sirens screamed through the streets.

"The chain will have to be shorter if you want the weight to get out far enough to keep him under." Dothan's voice was low.

"Make it shorter then." A helicopter rose into the sky, its spotlight scanning the ground below, starting at the safe house. Bartlett watched it for a moment, obviously uncomfortable with the delay. "Just get him out there before someone comes and sees him go."

Dothan nodded and the chain was adjusted accordingly. Jason was positioned on his knees with his back to the water, and his captors reluctantly released their hold on him. Dothan picked up the weight and swung it slowly from side to side, building momentum.

In the distance they heard sirens screaming through the dark streets.

"Get it out there," Bartlett ordered.

Dothan swung it back once more, then flung it with all his might into the darkness. The other men caught him as the momentum almost carried him off the end of the long dock. Jason's face struck the rough wood of the dock as he was jerked backwards into the water. In an instant he was gone.

"That was a good angle, Dothan," Bartlett told him as they strode away from the water. He turned to the men who held Kora's forearms. "Take her away. Use the route I marked out for you, and don't mess this up. I've invested a lot to get this girl."

They nodded and hurried her off toward the van as the light from the helicopter swept toward The Lake.

———

Jason struggled against the chains in the darkness. He could feel the pressure on his lungs and the realization came to him that as invincible as his body was, he still needed air to live.

"Lord, I need another chance. I can't die. Not after what I've done." Jason felt his feet touch the river bed. The chain between his hands and feet jerked him backwards as he shoved off the bottom, killing his upward thrust and causing him to fall short of the much needed oxygen. He let a little air out to relieve some of the pressure on his lungs. Words raced through his head as he begged God for a chance to undo what he had foolishly done. He jerked and twisted against the chains, the water making his movements worthlessly slow.

The pressure increased and Jason's struggles decreased. His mind drifted in and out of consciousness, and he dreamed he felt something tugging on the chains.

THIRTEEN

Benjamin burst through the surface of the water gasping for air then dove under for what felt like the hundredth time. He located the chain once more, the sharp metal where he had been cutting sliced into his fingers but he ignored the pain. Placing the cutters on the chain, he pressed them together with all his might. They did not seem to move at first, then the last of the thick chain gave in and the blades met. Benjamin discarded the cutters and grabbed the chain to pry the link apart. His lungs burned but he did not dare to stop. Roper had gone limp and Benjamin knew he did not have much time. The link twisted and Benjamin jerked it from the chain. He grabbed Roper and sprung off the bottom, gasping and choking as he burst through the surface once more. He felt desperately for Roper's head and pulled it above the surface.

"Come on, Roper," Benjamin gasped. He maneuvered Jason's limp body so his left arm was over Jason's shoulder and under his right arm. Swimming sideways with his right arm, Benjamin managed to keep them both above the surface of the water.

They were nearing the shore when Benjamin noticed the shadowy figure on the bank. He paused, treading water as silently as he could as he attempted to make out the stranger's features. Benjamin's breathing was heavy and he knew the stranger could hear it in the stillness of the night.

The sirens that had been screaming through the city were silent now and he wondered if they were the ones waiting for him. Benjamin's muscles were tired and Jason's limp body was slipping from his grasp. He pushed forward toward the shore. It didn't matter who was waiting for them, he had to get Roper breathing again.

The man stood silently as Benjamin approached. The moon had not risen and the darkness was only broken by a single streetlight in the lot behind the stranger. He stood above them, a silhouette, which neither moved nor spoke as Benjamin pulled Roper up the sloping bank.

Keeping an eye on the man, Benjamin rolled Roper onto his back and placed his hands together just under his ribcage. He gave Roper three sharp thrusts with the palm of his hand and water spewed from Roper's mouth. Benjamin scrambled to turn him over as Roper coughed and gagged on the water. After a few minutes Roper's body relaxed and he lay limp on the grass, his breathing rough but audible. Benjamin sighed and sat back on his heels.

"You are under arrest."

Benjamin started. He had nearly forgotten about the stranger. Now the man stood over him with a gun aimed at his chest.

Benjamin didn't respond. He dropped his eyes back to Roper and took a deep breath, still trying to recover from his dive.

"Put your hands together behind your back," the man's voice was quiet but firm.

"And if I don't?" Benjamin asked softly. The stranger had his back to the light so Benjamin still could not see his face.

"I don't need any trouble from you. He's the guy we're after. You will probably be released once you answer a few questions."

"I don't want to come along," Benjamin told him, standing

slowly. "Neither does he."

"He tell you that?" the man was being a little too nice, and Benjamin wondered why.

"Do I know you?"

There was a smile in the man's voice when he answered. "I don't believe so."

"Then just blast me and take him," Benjamin paused then added dully. "You're a cop aren't you?"

The man didn't respond.

"What do you have against me? I haven't done anything."

"You saved him. The chief will want to know why."

"Yeah?" Benjamin was aggravated. "Well, what if I don't know why? I don't have anything to say to your chief, or you. So the dude was stuck in the water and I got him out. Big deal. He's invincible isn't he? It's not like he would have died. I just think he…It's better for everyone if he's not stuck in the lake."

"Is that why you had to pump the water out of him?"

"If you put a bucket under water it fills up but it doesn't die." Benjamin countered. He knew if this got out there would be a lot of people coming to try their hand at drowning Roper.

The man nodded. "True. So you'll let me take him?"

Benjamin shrugged, "Be my guest."

The stranger hesitated as if sizing up Benjamin then he nodded and pulled out his radio. "I've got the suspect in custody at…"

Benjamin struck him hard, knocking him to the ground, and kicked the gun from his hand. Snatching up the gun, Benjamin stood over him, pointing the weapon at the man's back. "Alright, it's your turn. On your stomach." Benjamin used his foot to help him obey. "Alright, move toward the water."

The man started to rise but Benjamin shoved him back down with his foot.

"On your belly."

The man scooted slowly toward the water's edge.

Benjamin retrieved the radio and tossed it into the lake. "That's far enough."

Dropping to one knee beside Roper, Benjamin looped his arm under Roper's arms and lifted him to a sitting position, Roper sagged against him.

"Keep facing the water," Benjamin ordered, and the officer obeyed. "He's not a bad guy," Benjamin informed the stranger, as he worked out a way to carry Roper while he was still hog tied with chains. "So, he made a couple of mistakes. He'll make it right if you guys will stay out of his way."

"You're making a bad choice," the officer responded. "He's not a hero anymore. He has given up his standards and he'll just go down from here if we don't stop him."

"That's not true." The chains were proving to be unmanageable, and his cutters were somewhere on the bottom of the lake. There was no feasible way to carry his friend while he was wrapped in chains. Benjamin was running out of time again. "If you help me…" Benjamin hesitated. "If I can get him to the car, I promise you he'll make it right."

"You just happened to pull him out?" the officer asked, pushing himself up onto his elbows.

"Man, why do you cops have to make everything so hard?" Benjamin was at the end of his patience. The stress of almost losing his friend, and the realization that he was powerless to help him more, threatened to overwhelm him. Benjamin's eyes narrowed. He checked the gun, and found it was fully loaded. Rolling Roper onto his stomach, Benjamin aimed carefully for the chain and squeezed the trigger. The resounding boom echoed out across the lake. Benjamin blinked, blinded for a moment from the muzzle flash. The officer pressed himself against the grass, waiting for a second bullet to find its mark in his back.

Sticking the gun in his belt, Benjamin kept an eye on the cop as he worked the broken link from the chain between Roper's wrists. Benjamin pulled the cop's gun out once more and rolled Roper onto his back. His arms were free, but the chain between his ankles remained. Benjamin could not chance another shot. Keeping the officer covered, Benjamin moved closer to him and bumped the officer with his foot.

"Get up." Benjamin's tone was hard.

The man obeyed silently.

Benjamin could make out his features in the dim street-lights. He was a little shorter than Benjamin. His receding hairline and long thin nose gave him a look of experienced intelligence.

"Marshal?" The speaker was out of sight beyond the stand of trees.

"I'm here," Marshal responded before Benjamin could stop him.

Benjamin stepped back out of the light and into the shadow of a tree that stretched almost to the water's edge.

"You try anything and I'll fill you with lead," Benjamin informed him coldly, keeping the gun pointed at the officer. He had lived as a gangster for years and found it easy to slip back into that roll.

Marshal met his eyes without fear.

"I heard a shot," the speaker was coming toward them.

Marshal did not take his eyes from Benjamin. "I guess I'm a bit jumpy," he called to his partner.

Benjamin turned so he could see where the second man would emerge from the trees and dropped to one knee. "I'll shoot him if I see him," Benjamin warned.

"I'm alright, Hank. Stay on your beat," Marshal called.

Marshal's partner stopped immediately, hesitated and then moved away.

Benjamin waited until he could no longer hear Hank's

footsteps and then stepped from the shadows. "I mean what I said. If I see your partner, I'm going to let him have it."

"You won't see him," Marshal told him calmly.

"Pick him up." Benjamin nodded toward where Roper lay

"Where will you take him?" the man asked. There was no animosity in his tone.

"I'll deal with that, you just do it."

Marshal knelt and slid one arm under Roper's legs and the other behind his shoulders and with an involuntary grunt he lifted the limp body from the ground.

"Alright, you go first."

They reached the parking lot and Benjamin scanned the open space. There was no sign of Marshal's partner. "Keep right, and stay in the shadows."

"Right?"

Benjamin pressed the muzzle of the gun against the small of Marshal's back. "You have a problem with that?"

"No," Marshal answered calmly. He knew Benjamin was hanging on the brink of losing it, and was doing his best to keep him from going over. "You can use my car."

"I don't need your permission," Benjamin retorted. "Where are the keys?"

"In my left pocket."

The barrel pressed a little harder. "You'd better not be trying to trick me," Benjamin warned. Benjamin moved the gun so it pressed against the officer's rib cage. He pulled out the keys and scanned the lot once more.

"Your friend is getting very heavy," the officer said when Benjamin didn't move.

"Just see that you don't drop him." There was a cold threat in his tone.

Roper groaned a little and Benjamin's eyes left the shadows of the lot for a split second. He took a deep breath and let it out slowly before jabbing the officer in the back. "Go ahead. Walk slow and steady. If anything goes wrong, you'll go too. Got it?"

Marshal nodded, struggling under the dead weight of the fallen hero.

They crossed the space without interference but Benjamin did not let down his guard. He unlocked the car using the key and opened the back door.

He stood watch while the officer maneuvered Roper into the back seat, his eyes scanning the surrounding trees.

"He's in," the man informed him quietly.

"Good. Go around and get in the passenger seat."

The officer looked surprised but obeyed. Benjamin was in the driver's seat before the officer had gone around the car. He got in and waited while Benjamin started the car and put it into gear.

They pulled out of the lot and sped down the dark streets. Benjamin could tell the man was keeping track of their route. After five minutes of driving Benjamin pulled up to a curb beside a deserted building.

"Get out."

"Where will you go?"

One side of Benjamin's mouth went up in amusement. "You'll hear from us again. I told you, he'll make it right. Thanks for giving him another chance."

Marshal looked back at Roper and then at Benjamin. "Don't make me regret it."

Fourteen

Benjamin pulled into the exit of a large parking garage and found a place part way up the ramp.

"Roper?" There was no response. He shut off the engine and climbed into the back seat. "Come on, man, we don't have time for this." Benjamin shook Jason gently.

Peering out of the car he saw a lone police man enter the garage. "How did they get here so fast?" he demanded. Benjamin had hoped parking in a garage full of cars would buy him more time. He crawled back to the front seat and lay across the seats so his head was under the steering wheel. Working quickly he unclipped the fuse box cover, his fingers ran over the fuses and he jerked one out. Holding it up to the spear of light that came in the window he smiled and whispered. "Good bye interior lights." He climbed carefully into the back once again careful not to make the car rock more than necessary. Opening the side door he slipped out and peered through the back window at the officer who was playing his flashlight over the cars one by one. He pulled Jason halfway out of the car before he noticed the chains on Jason's ankles. He glanced back at the officer who was moving slowly up the row of cars in their direction. He tried to push Jason back into the car but his limp wet body would not cooperate. Turning around carefully, and still supporting Jason's body, Benjamin backed up to the door and grabbed the chain attached to the cuffs on Jason's ankles. Using his friend's limp arms Benjamin pulled Jason onto his back. When he hunched over Benjamin could just manage to keep Jason's feet off the ground.

"Man, you could help a little," Benjamin groaned softly. He tucked the chain into his belt and moved toward the front of the car. Progress was painstakingly slow as Benjamin worked his way down the row, moving whenever the cop examined the cars in the opposite row. There was not a phone within two blocks of where he dropped Marshal off, but apparently Marshal's partner had not wasted any time pulling together a search party.

Benjamin found two cars that were parked close together and let Jason slide to the ground, cringing as the chains rattled loudly on the cement. Benjamin sighed with relief. The static chirping of the cop's radio had drowned out the sound. "This is Scott, I have Marshal's car." There was a static reply Benjamin could not make out and then the officer gave his location. It would not be long before the garage was flooded with cops.

With sweat pouring down his neck, Benjamin crossed Jason's arms to keep the chains off the ground and pulled him slowly underneath the badly parked car. Car lights lit up the entrance and he froze as several policemen got out and went to join the cop by Marshal's squad car.

Jason groaned and coughed. Benjamin jumped to cover Jason's mouth and inhaled sharply as his head hit the undercarriage of the car. He froze, holding Jason's mouth with one hand and his head with the other. Jason moved slightly, and then went limp again.

Benjamin watched intently as another police car pulled in.

"Where is she?" Jason mumbled.

Benjamin started again, once more knocking his head on the undercarriage. Jason's eyes were open now.

"Don't do that to me," Benjamin hissed. "You just about

gave me a heart attack."

"Where is she?" Jason asked again and Benjamin clapped his hand over Jason's mouth.

"We'll talk about it later," Benjamin told him in a barely audible whisper. "Just don't move."

Jason pulled his face away and lay still, his breathing uneven and shaky. Benjamin knew he was crying.

"Hello, Marshal. Scott here found your car about two minutes ago. It seems to have been recently abandoned."

Benjamin held his breath as the men passed, wishing Jason would follow his example.

"The strange thing is it seems to have been full of water. The driver's seat and the whole back seat are soaked." The officer informed him. "There is some water outside the back passenger door here, but we'll need more light to sort it out." Marshal didn't respond.

Benjamin's eyes grew wide, and he lifted his head as much as possible. To his horror a thin stream of water was slowly creeping toward the edge of the dark shadow they were hiding under. He lay back realizing how hopeless this was. There would be a clear trail to their hiding place. He kicked himself for not thinking of that sooner.

Jason sighed shakily and his breathing gradually grew steady again.

"I don't think more lights are necessary," Marshal told the other men. "They wouldn't be dumb enough to stay this close to the stolen car."

Benjamin frowned. Why would he do that? Was he really giving Roper another chance?

"Marshal." It was the policeman who had found the car.
"Yes, Scott?"

"Can I talk to you for a minute?"

"Sure." They moved a little further away from the other men which brought them very close to the car Benjamin and Jason were hiding under.

"What are you trying to do Marshal?" Scott asked in a fierce whisper. "You know they are in here."

Marshal was silent for a moment. "Scott, do you remember that case I helped you out on last week?"

Scott let his breath out hard.

"I need that favor you said you would do me," Marshal went on his voice low. "I'll take all the heat for it if it goes bad. But I don't think it will."

"Marshal, you're going to get me fired."

Marshal waited silently.

"Fine," Scott sighed again. "Consider my debt paid. I'll move the men out. He turned away from Marshal and raised his voice. "Alright, let's clear out. Marshal says this is a dead lead. You men scour the grounds outside to pick up footprints."

The men seemed a little disappointed.

"Meanwhile, I'll take my car back to the station and get it cleaned," Marshal told him. "Okay." Scott wasn't totally convinced. "I'll take a few men over to The Lake and fan out from there." He lowered his voice as the men went back to their cars. "I hope you made the right choice, Marshal. That Roper is basically an unstoppable weapon now that he's gone bad."

"I know." Marshal's tone was serious. "But I think there's something bigger happening here."

Scott shook his head. "There you go with that God stuff again."

Marshal put a hand on Scott's arm as he turned to leave. "Thanks a lot."

"Sure."

"Oh, and Scott?"

Scott turned to face him again. "Yeah?"

"Do you mind picking up Hank on the way?"

"He's the one that called in that your car was missing. I

think he's riding with unit four now."

"Good, thanks."

The garage cleared out fairly quickly as they all went back to their search. Marshal went to his car. Benjamin heard the motor start. It pulled out and passed them slowly, disappearing into the darkness.

Benjamin scooted out from under the car and pulled Marshal's gun from his belt. He raised himself until he could see over the cars. The garage was empty. He stepped out, from between the cars and walked a little ways up the ramp. There was no one in sight. Benjamin made his way back down to the car they had been hiding under.

"Roper, it's clear." He stooped to peer under the car. Jason was sound asleep, his face still wet with tears. "Come on, man. We've got to get out of here." He reached under and grabbed Jason's arm. The chains scraped loudly as Benjamin pulled him part of the way out from under the car. Jason's eyes blinked open and he scooted the rest of the way out. Benjamin helped him to his feet and then started for the exit.

Jason stumbled after him the chains drowning out all hopes of a stealthy escape. Benjamin doubled back and stopped Jason. Picking up the chain that had attached Jason's hands to his ankles, Benjamin handed it to him. "Try to keep the noise down will you?"

Jason took it but did not respond to Benjamin's attempt at humor. A car entered the garage and they crouched out of sight.

"How do you feel?" Benjamin whispered, peering after the car. Jason did not answer and Benjamin glanced at him.

Jason sat with his back against the wall. His head was bowed and his fingers were entwined in his hair. Benjamin touched his shoulder.

"Roper we've got to keep moving."

Jason didn't move and Benjamin noticed his shoulders

were shaking.

Benjamin shook him gently. "Come on, Roper, pull yourself together. If they catch you, you'll be no help to Kora."

Jason heaved a shaky sigh and got to his feet. Benjamin moved quickly down the remainder of the ramp and flattened himself against the wall. Two policemen were talking together across the street. A radio crackled and they hurried off down the street. Benjamin motioned to Jason and slipped around the corner. Jason stumbled after him. He felt tired and weak. The chain joining his ankles slowed his progress considerably. They slipped out of the garage and Benjamin sprinted along the building behind the row of thick hedges. Jason stumbled on the chain and fell hard. In an instant Benjamin was beside him helping him to his feet.

Benjamin glanced around. Pulling Marshal's gun from his belt, he eyed it for a moment and then shook his head. "We'll have to find something else to get those chains off. We can't chance a bullet here. The garage will just amplify the sound, and the cops are all over this area." He laid a hand on his friend's shoulder. "You alright?"

Jason shook his head and stumbled on. Benjamin grasped his forearm and walked beside him to steady him.

"How did I get here?" Jason asked softly.

"I saw them throw you in," Benjamin answered with a twinge of bitterness in his voice. He scanned the street before hurrying Jason across.

"Where is she?" Jason asked again when they were safe in the shadows once more.

"I don't know, Roper. They didn't say where they were taking her. We'll have to deal with that when the time comes."

"You should have saved her, not me," Jason told him.

Benjamin pulled Jason to a stop and met his eyes. They were full of sorrow and despair. "Wait here." Benjamin ran back across the street and Jason watched as he retraced their steps. He hesitated at the edge of the garage and then sprinted across the open lit area, disappearing into the shadows on the other side.

A few minutes later Jason saw him coming back, he crouched in the shadows as Benjamin crossed the street once more. "Okay, listen hard." Benjamin's breathing was heavy. "When they put you in the water you were drowning. Do you see what I'm saying? You need to stay away from water. A cop was waiting when I pulled you out, but he's the only one who knows that you almost died."

"What did you do to him?" Jason asked softly.

"What's it matter? I waved a gun at him. But listen, he let you go. He could have taken you, both of us, but he let us go."

"Why?" Jason asked. "Why didn't you just leave me there?"

"I don't know." Benjamin looked back toward the garage, still puzzled by what Marshal had done. He looked at Jason and laughed softly. "I mean I don't know why he let us go. I didn't leave you there because you made a big mistake and now you need to make it right."

"You knew Bartlett was lying."

Benjamin nodded. "Yeah, I caught on pretty quick."

"How?" Jason asked earnestly.

"We can't get into all that right now," Benjamin responded. "We've got to find a place to hide out till we can get a plan together. I've got a contact here, but he's out until tomorrow. We're pretty much on our own for tonight. Any ideas?"

Jason met his eyes again. "Benjamin, why are you helping me? I thought you ditched me when we got here."

Benjamin gave him a sad smile. "Sometimes there are things you have to do, to get other things done. I knew they wouldn't believe I wasn't working with you unless you did. Honestly, you believed it a lot easier than I thought you would."

"What else was I supposed to believe?" Jason asked.

"You gotta trust a little more." Benjamin pulled him down

as a car sped past and then helped him to his feet once more. "Now where do you suggest we hide out?"

"There's an old rundown place a couple of blocks from the Black's apartment," Jason suggested.

Benjamin smiled. "I know the place."

FIFTEEN

"Anything?" Bartlett asked as Pablo entered the room. "Nothing, she's quieter than a church mouse."

"We'll give her time. Keep the questions going. She can't hold out forever," Bartlett told him. When does Dothan go in?"

Pablo thought for a moment. "I think not for another thirty minutes."

"Good, tell him I want to see him."

"Right, boss, I'll send him in."

———

"You've been living here?" Jason asked when Benjamin rounded the house and moved a loose board aside to let Jason in.

"The price was right," Benjamin answered following him inside. "As long as I don't use any lights at night the neighbors don't mind."

Jason was silent.

"You okay?" Benjamin asked for what seemed like the hundredth time. He had not thought much about Jason dying, but when he almost did it hit Benjamin hard.

Jason nodded. "Yeah. Just tired I guess."

"You almost died. I guess that's a good enough excuse." Benjamin moved about comfortably in the darkness and soon returned with a pair of clothes and a threadbare blanket which he handed to Jason. "Here, change into these and we'll hang yours up to dry, I've got a window with a lovely draft.

Jason looked at the clothes, amused. "How exactly do you want me to get in them?" he pointed to the chains around his ankles.

Benjamin frowned. "We will have to deal with those."

Jason handed the clothes back, but kept the blanket. "You might as well change into them."

Benjamin took them and disappeared into another room, the floorboards creaking loudly as he crossed them.

"Mine should be dry in a few hours. The wind is coming in nice and strong tonight. I think the guy next door ought to have something that can cut through them. He's always out in that little shed running tools. That's where I got the cutters I got you out with. I knew they would be useful, so I kept them on hand. But we'll have to wait for the guy to go to work tomorrow. He's a real light sleeper."

"What did you think the clippers would be useful for?" Jason asked skeptically.

Benjamin shrugged and sat down against the far wall. "You never know. I wish I had kept my head enough to stick them in my pocket or something. You going all limp on me really shook me up. You've been a good friend to me, and I'm sorry for getting you into all this."

"It's not your fault, Benjamin. It was my own blundering naiveté." Jason wrapped the blanket around himself and sat with his knees against his chest.

"Caring and trusting are not signs of weakness," Benjamin told him seriously. "It takes more strength than living on your own and being your own boss. That's what crooks do. They use you, and then ditch you when things get hot. It's a lot harder to see it through. I helped you because you're my friend, I trust you with my life. The key is knowing when to trust and when to pull away."

"You were smart to leave," Jason told him.

"No, I shouldn't have. I used you as the decoy, and I broke the trust that was between us."

Jason did not answer.

"Roper, Toby was not like the other guys." Benjamin paused to find the right words. "He really cared. When things got hot he made sure we all got out instead of ditching us and making a break for it. That's why I had to come here."

"Did Toby send for you?"

"Not exactly, I knew something had happened to him, but I didn't know he had been killed. I knew when he left Frankford that if he didn't get the formula through it was my responsibility to finish the job for him. There was a lot you didn't see back in Frankford, a lot of underlying things going on that only a few of us were privy to. Even I wasn't supposed to know."

"Mrs. Black told me something about it."

"She probably didn't know the half of what was happening," Benjamin answered quietly.

"God used you to answer my prayer tonight," Jason told him after a long silence.

"How so?"

"When I was in the water, I knew I was dying, and I begged God for a chance to make it right. He used you to give it to me."

"And that Marshal guy," Benjamin added. "That was really strange for a cop."

They fell silent, lost in thought.

"I'll need to go see Mrs. Black," Jason said quietly.

"You're crazy. That place will be hopping with cops for the next few days."

"Somehow I need to let them know how sorry I am." Jason pulled the blanket closer around him.

"I'll get the message to them," Benjamin told him. "You've got to stay clear until we figure out where Kora is."

"Tell me what you know about what has happened."

Benjamin let his breath out slowly. "Yeah, you'll need to know sometime." He stretched out on the dirty carpet and folded his hands behind his head. "Territ was covering for Kora. Apparently she found Toby before Territ and I'm supposing she's the one he told about the formula. She was supposed to take it straight to the FBI but Bartlett's men closed in so quickly that she didn't have a chance. Territ didn't even get to go to Toby's funeral," Benjamin added. There was anger in his voice. "Bartlett or one of his men found Toby, and when he found out that Toby had stashed the formula they shot him. My guess is that one of Toby's friends was making things hot for them. They knew they didn't have time to get him to talk, so they shot him to keep things even."

"Bartlett said something about Toby having just gotten it from someone else."

Benjamin grunted in disgust. "That's just like him to twist the truth to make his lie more believable." The bitterness was back in Benjamin's voice and his tone was hard. "Mrs. Black told me Toby was tracking the man down for weeks, racing against Bartlett's men to get the document. From what Kora told them, Toby had swiped the document and was trying to get it to the agent."

"Bartlett?" Jason was confused.

"No, the real Bartlett was already very dead by that time. I guess the Bartlett we know is really some guy named James Maldolf. He bumped off the real agent and slipped right into his place without any fuss. The real Bartlett did a lot of field work and couldn't contact headquarters very often without blowing his cover, so the FBI didn't really see a big change in his communications with them. When they heard you had come here they sent an agent out to contact Bartlett but he failed to show up on two separate occasions. They have apparently had a man tracking him since then, hoping he would lead them to whoever has the formula."

"But I called them and the person I talked to said Bartlett was still working for them."

"Where did you call from?" Benjamin asked.

"The hotel."

Benjamin smiled regretfully. "They probably had your line rewired or something so you really never got through to them."

"Why didn't you tell me all this?"

"I tried, Roper. Remember the windows? I couldn't just blurt it out, there were people who would overhear and it would totally blow my cover."

"I wish you had blown it," Jason said quietly

"They were on the way to arrest Bartlett and didn't want him spooked," Benjamin answered. "I didn't realize it would take them so long to get to him. Besides, I thought you understood. I guess I thought you trusted me more."

Jason laid his head on his knees. "I totally blew it, Benjamin." His voice was full of sorrow.

"Yes, but now you are going to make it right," Benjamin answered firmly. "Here's the rest of it."

"What about Kora?"

"Kora really was in a safe house. We sent her there…"

"We?" Jason asked in surprise.

"Yes. Taroe sent some men to get her. You were being watched very closely by Bartlett's men which bought us a little more time."

"If I had only known," Jason groaned in anguish. "Why didn't I listen to you? Why didn't I listen to her?"

"Roper, pull yourself together," Benjamin told him bluntly. "Sure you blew it, but having an emotional breakdown isn't going to solve anything. I need you to pull yourself together and sort this out."

Jason was silent for a long time and Benjamin waited.

"What is the formula?" Jason's voice was steady again.

Benjamin shook his head. This wasn't going to be easy for Jason to hear. "It's the formula to make another you."

Jason frowned in the darkness. "What do you mean?"

"Your dad never gave up on recreating the compound that made you invincible," Benjamin responded. "A noted scientist worked for years with McCard to reproduce that compound. The formula he created, matched with the portion McCard had, was supposed to do the trick."

"So that is what this is all about?"

"Yes." Benjamin fell silent.

"There's more, isn't there?" Jason pressed.

Benjamin sighed. "Do you remember the big fuss about Taylor's store? That was because that is where one of us was supposed to meet the delivery man who was carrying the formula and deliver it to Jarris. The delivery was all set up but then Taylor chickened out and threatened to expose us after he'd already been paid off."

"That's why Jarris wanted Taylor out so badly."

"Yes, we made the raid on the store the night the delivery was supposed to be made but the cops showed up and screwed things up. Thanks to you, the handoff was delayed. The messenger pulled out and set up another meeting time, but when you blew open the gang he skipped town, taking the formula with him. Toby followed him back to his hometown, here, and worked day and night to get a hold of that document. He finally did, but Maldolf's men were right on him. From what we could tell from talking to Kora, he shook the man tailing him just long enough to stash the document and make a run for it."

"What was he going to do with it?"

"Turn it in, or destroy it, I guess," Benjamin answered. "Taroe said Toby was working as an agent for them all along. That is why he was in Frankford, to intercept that document.

Apparently things started getting out of hand just before you showed up. Jarris was aware there was someone on the inside working against him. He was watching Toby, all of us really. I was paid to squeal on the other men. I think you were hired for the same thing at first but then you know the rest."

"I wish Mrs. Black had told me all this."

"She has her kids to think of, Roper. They were really in a tight place."

Jason thought for a moment before responding. "What do you think our next step should be?"

Benjamin smiled. "You're the genius leader."

"I'm serious, Benjamin. I've totally screwed this mission while you were out saving everyone." Jason's chains clinked softly as he rubbed his face with his hands. "I should be your side-kick."

Benjamin laughed softly. "Okay, side-kick. I say we sleep tonight and start out new tomorrow."

"Where will we start?"

"On the corner of Fifth and Jasper."

"Where is that?"

"East of here, about four or five blocks."

"Do I just stand out on the corner?"

"Yeah, and go ahead and wave your chains around while you are at it," Benjamin laughed. "There is a pale yellow house on the corner. Go right in the gate on the side and let yourself in the back door. It will be unlocked."

"Okay."

"The only catch is, and this is what could foul it up, we can't show up until after 9:30. So the sun will already be up and the chances of being spotted are much higher. We will probably have to separate, but whatever happens I need you to meet me there."

Jason nodded. "Is that where your friend lives?"

"The contact, yes."

"How do you know it is safe?"

Benjamin shrugged. "Toby gave me his name. That's enough for me."

Sixteen

"Sergeant, I found Marshal's gun." The rookie used a handkerchief to pull it from the bushes. "They must have ditched it here as they passed." He stood with his back to the garage and squinted down the street. Before him the sky was slowly lightening, framing the dark buildings with its thin light. "Where do you think they would be hiding?"

"What makes you think they are hiding?" the Sergeant asked joining him and taking the gun. "These are experienced men, not petty crooks."

"They could be rooming in any one of those hotels." The rookie continued, pointing out the hotels in sight.

The Sergeant laughed. "Or...," he turned the rookie in the opposite direction toward the buildings still shrouded in darkness.. "They could have thrown it here to throw you off. Like I said, Roper is experienced and knows what he's doing. Only an inexperienced crook will throw away a gun along his escape route. Roper is not inexperienced. This was planted, not hidden."

The rookie was obviously impressed. "So they...," he waited while the Sergeant called in their find.

"For now, Perry, we are looking for only one man," the Sergeant told him as they walked back to the car. "Marshal said nothing about a second man being involved."

Perry nodded.

"We will concentrate our search on the west end of town.

My guess is that is where he will be."

––––––

The blackness of the night had faded into a dark gray-ish light that seeped in through the cracks in the shuttered windows. Jason sat up slowly and flipped the blanket off. He could make out Benjamin still asleep across the room. Jason found the length of chain attached to his ankles and rose softly, keeping the chain taut so it would not rattle as he walked. Benjamin moved slightly as Jason reached for his gun. Waiting until he was still again, Jason shoved Benjamin's gun into his own belt. He pushed aside the board Benjamin had used for a door and slipped out into the yard.

Jason paused and took a deep breath of the still air. "Thank you, Lord, for life," he whispered. He stood there a moment more, enjoying the stillness, then moved away from the house. The man next door was obviously a bit better off than those around him. His house was surrounded by a new privacy fence. Jason made his way to the large tree that hung over the fence line and reached up, brushing his fingertips on the underside of the branch. He smiled. It was just the right height. Wrapping the loose chain around his ankle Jason secured it there and then jumped up, catching the branch easily. He pulled himself up and swung his knee over the branch, shimmying along its length until he was past the fence. He paused, looking over the yard below him. The grass was short and the flowerbeds well-manicured. The workshop Benjamin had told him about was across the yard and had a well laid stone path that connected it to the house. The house itself was dark inside. He gripped the branch and slid his legs off, dropping to the ground. He landed awkwardly, catching himself with his hands, and crouched there, watching the house. Nothing moved inside. He moved silently to the workshop, and noticed an infant swing hanging from another branch of the tree.

So this was not just a single man. There was a family living here. Jason glanced at the house again. That could complicate things, or make them easier depending on how he worked it.

He whispered a prayer as he reached for the door knob. It was open. "Thank you, Lord," he breathed, slipping inside. Pulling the door shut, he waited for his eyes to adjust to the darkness. There was a light switch beside the door, but Jason felt his way forward, hoping there was a lamp of some kind he could use instead of the main light. As his eyes adjusted to the darkness he could make out a small lamp at the end of the bench. He switched it on, squinting at the sudden brightness. The workshop was very well kept. The tools all hung in neat rows on peg boards that lined the walls. He fingered a file set then spotted a pair of bolt cutters on the opposite wall. With a sigh he hung the file set back on its hook and quickly crossed the room. His foot caught on an extension cord and he stumbled, trying frantically to catch himself. As he fell his hand struck something and a jar of nails crashed to the floor. Jason scrambled to his feet and grabbed the cutters. He didn't need to look to know the noise had woken the shop's owner.

Jason pulled out Benjamin's gun and laid it on the floor beside him. He placed the cutters around the cuff on his ankle and pressed them closed.

He was twisting off the second cuff when he heard the house door open slowly. Jason pulled the cuff off and picked up Benjamin's gun. He moved to stand beside the door. If this guy was like most frightened homeowners, his gun would be the first thing to enter the shop.

A few moments later the barrel of a .22 appeared. Jason grabbed it, twisting it easily out of the man's hand while stepping around so the man could see his gun.

They looked at each other for a moment. The man, who wore a robe over his pajamas, was in his late thirties and in good physical condition. His eyes, blue and piercing, met Jason's without fear.

"What are you doing here?" he asked. Spotting the chains on the floor, his eyes darted back to Jason's face. "You are the guy the police are after."

"Eli, is everything alright?" a woman called from the house.

"Tell her everything is fine," Jason told him quietly. "And make it believable. If she calls the cops you are toast."

"Its fine, Lisa," Eli called. "Nothing to worry about, I'll be right in."

"You have a kid, right?" Jason asked keeping the gun trained on him.

Eli met Jason's eyes. There was a warning in his look that was tainted by fear.

Jason silenced him with a wave of his gun. "Don't start all that, I'm not going to hurt him, or any of you if you cooperate."

"What do you want?" Eli asked, his face hard.

"I need your help," Jason answered. "I'm really sorry to have to do this to you. But I'm in a tight spot."

"What do you want?" Eli asked again, not at all sympathetic.

"The cutters are over there."

Eli retrieved them without a word.

Moving to the work bench, Jason placed his left wrist on the bench, keeping Eli covered. "Cut it off."

Eli eyed him suspiciously.

"Hurry up with it," Jason commanded. "I don't have all night."

"You'll have a lot of time on your hands once they catch you," Eli responded, sliding the blade of the cutter under the cuff.

"They can do whatever they want to me after I free the girl," Jason answered.

Eli cut the first cuff and twisted it off.

Jason moved around him to the other side and switched the gun to his left hand, laying his right on the bench.

"What girl?" Eli asked putting the cutter in place.

"Kora Black."

Eli looked up in surprise. "But didn't you just kidnap her?"

"Yes, and if there was any way to go back and undo it I would." Jason felt the sorrow welling up again and pushed it back. "Well, hurry up and cut it."

Eli obeyed and twisted the cuff off. "So why did you do it?"

"There's all kinds of excuses I could give." Jason switched the gun back to his right hand. "The truth is, I stopped trusting the ones who had proved I could trust them. I did what I thought was right without seeking counsel."

Eli looked at him, unsure if he should believe him or not.

"I messed up," Jason told him bluntly. "So now I've put her in danger, ruined my reputation and got myself a task that seems bigger than I can do." Jason laughed. "I have no idea why I am telling you all this. I'm sorry, you're free to go. I'll put your gun on your workbench once you're inside."

Eli nodded, a slight frown creased his brow as he hung up the clippers and opened the door. Blue and red police lights flashed across the yard.

"There's a policeman coming this way," Eli informed him.

Jason grabbed the cuffs and shoved them out of sight. "I knew she would call..."

"It wasn't Lisa." Eli cut him off quickly. "She wouldn't have called them."

"I'll let it go if you get rid of this cop," Jason told him, backing into the shadows. "Tell them I'm not here."

"Sir, you're working awfully early, is everything alright?" the officer asked.

"Yes, I was just grabbing something," Eli told him, aware of the gun behind him. "Is everything okay?"

"Yes, we are doing a routine search next door and didn't want to alarm you. I was going to go to the house but I saw your light was on out here."

"Who are you looking for?"

"Like I said, I don't want to alarm you. We have reason to believe that the kidnapper, Jason Roper, is hiding out in this area. Have you seen the bulletins on him?

"Yes, my wife and I saw it last night."

"Good, then I don't have to tell you he is a dangerous person. If you see or hear anything don't hesitate to call us."

Eli nodded and reached in to turn out the lamp. "Thank you for letting me know."

———

Benjamin's eyes flicked open. The room was illuminated with the familiar flashing of police lights. He reached for his gun, but it was gone. Benjamin sat up quickly. His eyes darted to where Jason had been sleeping. Only the blanket he had used remained. Benjamin smiled and lay back down. He knew the police were surrounding the house but he had nothing to hide. Moments later the dilapidated door burst open, boards and splintered wood flew into the room. Benjamin scrambled to his feet in mock surprise as police flooded the room, training their guns on Benjamin as they entered. Benjamin raised his hands slowly and placed them on his head with his fingers entwined. Two officers stayed to cover him while the others searched the house.

"There's no one else here."

Benjamin relaxed. "That's a relief."

"Why?" One of the officers moved forward.

"Because I don't want people coming and going while I'm sleeping," Benjamin told him pointedly. He stooped and pulled his backpack toward him.

"Drop it," the officer yelled, jabbing at Benjamin with

his gun.

Benjamin obeyed, watching as they dug through his bag and then dumped its contents onto the dirty carpet. One of them looked at him and held up a handful of loose bullets.

"What are these?"

"Bullets," Benjamin answered with a half smile.

"Get your hands up," the officer commanded loudly.

Benjamin relaced his fingers on his head.

"Where's your gun?"

"I don't have one," Benjamin lied easily.

The officer did not find his answer amusing. "Search him."

Another officer came forward, keeping out of his partner's line of fire as he patted down Benjamin's clothes. He pulled out a small lock picking kit and a folded pocket knife before backing away. "There's nothing else on him."

"Where's the gun?"

"I don't have a gun," Benjamin repeated.

"You have half a case of bullets rolling around in your bag," the officer pointed out. "Don't expect me to believe you keep them all for good luck. I'm going to ask you one more time. Where is your gun?"

"I sell the bullets," Benjamin confessed, meeting the accusing eyes of the officer. "I have a supplier and can get them cheap. Then I sell them around town."

"Who do you sell them to?"

Benjamin snorted in distain. "Like I'd tell you. You don't belong here, and you've got no right barging in here like you own the place. I didn't do anything illegal." He took his hands down and they did not object. "Can I get my things?"

"We'll hang on to the bullets but you're free to take the rest." The officer was hoping to soften Benjamin's defensive attitude. "How long have you been here?"

"As in tonight or nights total?" Benjamin asked stuffing his clothes back into the bag.

"Tonight."

"What time is it?" he asked.

"Five thirty," the officer told him.

"Then I've been here all night," Benjamin lied freely. "Alone," he added when they did not respond.

"What about these pants we found in the other room?" another officer brought them to him.

"They're mine." Benjamin did not even look at them.

"Why were they drying by the window?"

"Because that's where the wind comes in."

The officer glared at him. "We want to know why they were wet in the first place."

Benjamin retrieved Jason's blanket and set to work rolling it. "Because sometimes things I wear get dirty, then I wash them, and hang them up for the wind to dry," Benjamin answered in a derisive tone.

"Don't get fresh." The officer was losing his patience. "Where's Roper?"

"Is that who you are looking for?" Benjamin swung his backpack onto his shoulder and grinned at him. "How should I know where he is? I ditched that loser when I got here."

"Is that so? Then I guess we'll have to take you in." The officer nodded to his partner who grabbed Benjamin's arm and slapped a cuff onto his wrist.

"What! Why?" Benjamin tried to pull away. "I haven't done anything wrong."

The policeman shoved him against the wall, pulling Benjamin's backpack from his back and cuffing his hands behind him.

"What do you think you're doing?" Benjamin protested as they moved him toward the door. "I've cooperated with you."

"We'd like to ask you a few more questions downtown." The officer replied. "You're story doesn't quite line up. Bring his things."

Seventeen

Jason pushed open the door of the small thrift shop and ran a hand over his hair. He had combed it forward and it now hung like bangs in his face. He stuck out his lower jaw creating the illusion of an under bite and walked with his shoulders slightly hunched.

"Good morning." The lady at the desk was wearing the most obnoxious shirt Jason had ever seen. Long chains of costume jewelry completed her unique outfit. She was leaning on the counter talking in hushed tones to a white-haired lady on the other side.

"Hi," Jason mumbled, walking to the men's section. He found a button up shirt and a pair of baggy jeans. "Where's your changing room?" Jason asked her from across the store.

"In the back, past the shoes," She answered without looking up.

Jason slipped into the small room and pulled the clothes over his own. He pulled a five dollar bill out of his damp wallet and crumpled it into a small ball. He smoothed it out a little and then stuffed it into the pocket of the jeans, pushing the door open, he hesitated. There was a policeman at the counter. The owner nodded seriously as the officer spoke, and the white haired lady was leaning in to catch what he was saying. Jason checked his appearance in the mirror once more and let his breath out slowly. "Alright Lord, here it goes." He pushed open the door and walked to the counter.

The officer acknowledged him and Jason nodded back making it look as awkward as possible. "Didja catch that kidnapper dude?" he asked, allowing a little excitement into his tone.

"No, not yet." The officer smiled patronizingly. "But we'll get him." He turned his attention back to the lady behind the counter. "I'll see you later Gertrude. Let me know if you see anything."

Gertrude smiled at him. "Will do."

She moved away from the other lady, who stood staring at Jason as if he had just walked out of a celebrity show.

"What can I do for you?" Gertrude asked politely.

"I wanna get these clothes, does it matter if I wear them out? I don't really wanna be seen in the old things I came in with," Jason told her truthfully.

"I don't have a problem with that. It's just the pants and shirt right?"

"Yeah." He picked up a pair of sunglasses from a rack by the counter. "How much are these?"

"Those will go very nicely with your new outfit," the other lady told him.

Jason gave her a little embarrassed smile, hoping he would not be stuck with an underbite for life.

"Fifty cents," Gertrude told him with a wink at her friend. "Do you want them?"

"Yeah." Jason put them on the counter.

"That will be five dollars even," she told him, adjusting her gaudy necklace.

Jason dug in his pocket, pulled out the crumpled bill and slid it across the counter.

She put it into the register and handed him the hand-written receipt.

"Have a good day."

"You too," Jason replied.

Sliding the sunglasses into place, he pushed open the door and walked down the sidewalk toward the lake.

———

"What about your shoes. Why are they wet?" the officer demanded, slapping them onto the table in front of Benjamin.

Benjamin looked at them and then at the officer. He was seated in a plain wooden chair in a small room that was unfurnished except for his chair and the table his shoes were on.

"Well?" the officer asked again.

Benjamin sighed and answered in a bored tone. "My shoes are wet because I spilled mop water on them. It's not hard to figure that out since that is the reason my pants were drying."

"My men tell me there was mud and the type of algae you find in a lake on your pants and shoes. Do you usually mop with pond water?"

Benjamin sat back and crossed his arms. "No."

"Listen, Bub, your story stinks. The facts don't line up."

Benjamin shrugged.

"We've got all the time in the world." The officer sat on the edge of the table and crossed his arms. "Let me know when you are ready to tell me where you really were."

Benjamin did not have time for this. "Alright, I didn't tell you because I knew you would try to pin this whole kidnapping deal on me. So I slipped in the lake, and it happened to be on the same day Roper turns bad."

"Tell me about your slipping."

"I had a rough morning at work, things aren't exactly harmonious between myself and some of the uppity guys who like to step on me. So I took a walk yesterday, to kind of get away and cool off."

"Around the lake?" the officer asked.

"Yeah, I was on the path mostly but I saw something in the water and went over to check it out."

"What was it?"

Benjamin looked embarrassed. "It was just a piece of trash, but I didn't know that until after I slipped on the bank and fell in." Benjamin did not meet the officer's eyes. He waited a moment, then added, "I did use mop water to try to get the grunge off."

"Anything else you'd like to add?"

"I knew if I told you guys I was at the lake you would all go wild and say I was the one who was helping Roper. What I told you about ditching him was true. We weren't working together."

"How did you know we would make that connection?"

"I knew you cops were all searching around the lake for stuff to connect to the case since that's where Roper's car was. So I knew me being there would just incriminate me."

"So you weren't there last night?" he asked.

Benjamin met his eyes without flinching. "No, I wasn't."

"Your coworkers said you ran out pretty quickly when you heard about Roper," the officer observed skeptically. "What's your excuse for that?"

Benjamin shrugged again. "Same reason. You knew where I worked and I didn't want to get picked up for his job."

Benjamin could tell he was not convinced.

Someone knocked on the door and the officer stepped out. He returned a moment later, taking his seat on the table once more.

"It would have made my job a lot easier if you had leveled with me at the first."

"I'm done taking his raps for him," Benjamin answered quietly.

"As far as I can tell you won't take it this time. There are a few facts we will have to verify before we let you go but I don't think it will take long."

"It doesn't really matter," Benjamin answered bitterly.

"I probably don't have a job to be late for anymore thanks to Roper."

———

Jason set the bottle of Elmer's glue and a comb on the counter and waited as the cashier scanned it. He had chosen a chunky teenager who was beebopping slightly to music only he could hear.

"Two twelve." The casher did not even glance up at him.

Jason handed him the money and took his bag. "Do you have a restroom?"

"It's in the back." The cashier gestured vaguely toward the back of the store.

"Thanks." Jason walked through the aisles and looked across the back wall spotting the bathroom to his right. He made a bee line for it and locked the door behind himself. He looked at his reflection in the dirty mirror, opened the bottle of glue, and squeezed it out in a zig-zag pattern across the top of his head. Using the comb he worked it into his hair, combing it forward and into his face. He smoothed the rest of his hair down then waited a moment before testing it. Unsatisfied he repeated the process. His hair was stiffening nicely. He looked himself over in the mirror and took a deep breath. He pushed open the door and walked through the store and out the front door. He walked a few streets away before stuffing the bag into a large trash can. Checking his watch, he moved down the street. He still had some time to kill before he headed for the contact's house.

Jason kept walking so he would blend with the other pedestrians, Benjamin's gun resting snuggly against him and out of sight. He looked up and noticed he was just down the street from the hotel where he had been staying. He stopped walking and looked around. The apartment complex where the Black's lived was just around the corner. He moved toward it, knowing what he was doing could blow their whole plan, yet needing to do it. He skirted the complex keeping his gait slow and casual as he walked past the familiar sights. Benjamin was right. There were policemen on every corner and several strolled purposefully through the complex.

Jason noticed his car had been towed from The Lake parking lot and wondered how he would get his backpack. He had a limited supply of invincible clothes and did not care to lose them. A quick movement to his right caught his eye and he turned to see what it was.

Sammis stood several yards away, his dark eyes locked on Jason. Jason met his gaze but did not slow his pace.

Two blocks later Jason stopped and pretended to fix his shoe lace. A few minutes later Sammis strolled by. He picked up a rock and tossed it into the street. "I know who you are," he told Jason without looking at him.

"I know," Jason answered, still fiddling with his shoe.

"Raquel hates you."

"I deserve it."

"I told him you were going to get Kora out." Sammis looked at Jason and there was a pleading in his expression.

"I am," Jason answered standing up and brushing something invisible off his jeans. "I need you to tell your mother."

"You made her cry."

Jason cringed at the boy's accusing tone. "I know, Sammis. I made a really big mistake." Jason glanced around to make sure no one was watching them. "I asked the Lord to give me a chance to make it right, and He did. Now I need you to tell your mom that I am going to help Kora. I need you to tell her so that no one else will hear or else they will all come trying to catch me and I will not be able to get to Kora to help her." Jason looked into Sammis' wizened face. "Will you do that for me?"

"Do you promise to help Kora?"

Jason did not hesitate. "I promise."

EIGHTEEN

Jason pushed the decorative gate open, and walked into the back yard as if he owned it. His eyes darted around the enclosure. The grass grew tall close to the fence line but the sporadic clumps of grass scattered across the dirt yard were well trimmed. A large oak tree overshadowed almost the entire area making it cool and dim though the sun had been up for hours.

Jason scanned the overhanging branches and then moved silently toward the back door of the house. He had the eerie sensation of being watched, but saw no sign of life around him. Turning the knob he found the door was unlocked, as Benjamin had predicted, and pushed it open. The shadowy yard made it easy to make out the dim interior of the house. An easy chair sat beside the entrance of the hall to his right, and a couch took up the majority of the wall to his left. Straight ahead there was a small dining room table with four matching chairs arranged neatly around it. Beyond that, Jason could see the start of an open tiled area he guessed was the kitchen.

"Hello?" Jason called softly. He stood outside the door, not wanting to go inside.

After a few minutes of silence Jason moved into the room keeping the door open. He reached for Benjamin's gun and was rewarded by a movement from the dark hallway.

"There's no need for that. Come on in." The man moved

to where Jason could see him. He was a little under six foot, and in his hand was a short barreled shotgun.

Jason closed the door behind him and waited.

"So you're the infamous Jason Roper?" His short light colored hair was tight with curls, and his green eyes sparkled with amusement. "I like the new look."

Jason self-consciously ran his hand across his stiff hair.

"You've caused quite a ruckus in this little town." Eddie sat in the easy chair and pulled up the footrest, the shotgun resting comfortably across his lap. "Have a seat. What do you prefer to go by, Jason or Roper?"

"Roper," Jason answered sitting on the couch. The man's laidback manner pushed away his uneasiness.

"That's fair enough. I'm Eddie Shartell, but I go by Eddie. Little more personal. But," Eddie shrugged, "it is purely preference in this business. Benjamin tells me you want to get Kora out of Maldolf's hands.

"That's right. He said you could help me."

Eddie laid aside the shotgun and got up. "I've done a little studying on it and I think we can pull it off." He disappeared into the bedroom and returned with a bulging folder. "We'll have to wait for Benjamin to go over all this since we don't have time to do it twice. He should be here soon, but since they just released him he'll have to take a round-about route."

"So the police did get him."

"Yeah, they picked him up this morning, around five or so." Eddie put the file on the table. "Gave him some cell time, questioned him a bit, and let him go. That Benjamin has a smooth tongue. Trust me, he can talk his way out of anything."

"How do you know they released him?" Jason asked.

Eddie shrugged. "It pays to know what's going on with your people. Do you want something to drink? Nothing alcoholic though, I don't believe in the stuff."

Jason grinned. "I'm fine, thanks."

"Well then, let's get down to business." Eddie checked the street and then slid the wooden coffee table out of the center of the room. "Do you mind pulling up that rug?"

Jason rose and grasped the edge of the decorative rug, pulling it toward the kitchen, and laying it over the coffee table. Underneath was a large rectangle of well-polished wood.

"This is where I keep my babies," Eddie told him proudly. He produced a key and pulled two locks from between the wood and the carpet. Once they were unlocked, he reverently lifted the lid revealing a diverse collection of gleaming weapons.

Jason looked at Eddie and smiled. Eddie looked like a proud father showing off his well-behaved children.

Eddie chose a Glock and handed it to Jason. "It's not a 23 like your old one, but it takes the same caliber bullets so you can use what you already have."

"I don't have any bullets," Jason told him. "The only gun I have is Benjamin's."

Eddie shook his head as if Jason had missed something obvious. "The ones in your backpack are .40, this takes .40." He held the gun out to Jason.

"I don't have my backpack."

"I have your backpack. Just take the gun, Roper." Eddie reached out and took Jason by the wrist, placing the gun in his hand. "You're acting like I'm handing you a time bomb."

Jason held onto the Glock and Eddie released his wrist. "How did you get my backpack?"

"You can pay me back later." Eddie chose a gun and slipped it into the shoulder holster beneath his jacket. "Let's see what Benjamin uses."

Jason pulled it out and handed it to Eddie who shook his head sadly.

"He has got to invest in some oil. This thing is as dry as

a desert." Eddie handed it back and selected two more guns. "Do you like one or two?"

"I guess I would be more prepared with two."

Eddie grinned. "Now you're starting to think." He handed Jason a second Glock and a folded knife. "That ought to keep you busy enough." He used a key to open a smaller wooden box and pulled out four boxes of shells from inside.

"I don't expect we will need more than two, but luck favors the prepared."

Jason smiled, thinking of Benjamin. He watched silently as Eddie closed the wooden boxes, carefully locking each one.

"I'll let you get the rug again," Eddie told him, putting the guns in a row on the couch.

"Aren't you afraid the police will find all that?" Jason asked letting the rug fall into place.

"No." Eddie smiled. "What reason do they have to look? You see, the police are there to help the good people and catch the bad people. I help them now and then and they do what they do and let me do what I do. I'm not involved in anything illegal per say and they enjoy the tips I give them, so we get along quite nicely." Eddie laughed. "Don't get all nervous. I'm not going to turn you in." He fell silent. Tilting his head slightly he stood motionless, listening to something Jason could not hear.

Eddie came to life once more with a cheerful smile. "Here's Benjamin now."

Jason followed him to the table and watched as he opened the file. He unfolded a blueprint of a building and laid it out along with a geographical map and several inside shots of the building.

"How did you get all this?" Jason asked in awe.

Eddie grinned, enjoying Jason's amazement. "It's not what you have in this business, it's who you know."

———

"Marshal, the Chief wants to see you." Hank held the office door open for Marshal to follow him.

"What's up?" Marshal asked rising from his desk.

"Come on, Marshal. You and I both know there's more to your story than what you told the Chief."

Marshal walked past Hank into the hall. "I think I told him all the pertinent facts."

"And what about the not so pertinent ones?" Hank put his hand on Marshal's arm and Marshal turned to face his partner. "I've been your partner for three years now. Don't you think I know you a little better than that?"

Marshal grinned and slapped Hank on the back. "Yes. You are a good man, Hank." He turned and continued down the hall.

Hank hurried to catch up with him. "Marshal, the Chief isn't happy with you."

"Yeah, I kind of figured I'd take some heat for it."

"For what?" Hank asked almost eagerly.

Marshal laughed. "Hank, you never could stand a little mystery."

"Well, at least let me in on it." Hank said, pulling him to a stop once more just outside the Chief's door.

"And incriminate my innocent partner? I wouldn't think of it." Marshal grinned at Hank's annoyed look.

"Come on in, boys," the Chief called and they pushed open the door. "Have a seat. Hank, you can pull that chair over here." The Chief gestured to a chair in the corner. Hank retrieved it and sat beside Marshal.

"Marshal, I can't help but think you are holding out on us." The Chief was a tall broad-shouldered man with thick gray hair and a wide mustache. His eyes were kind but serious as he looked at the men seated before him.

"What exactly makes you think that?" Marshal was just

as serious.

"Marshal, it doesn't take a rocket scientist to know that there was more than one man in your car. There were two seats wet and a very clear water trail from your car. Why did you send the men out of the garage?"

"Sir, I know what I did was out of line, but I didn't have time to contact you for permission. There were two people in my car that night, and I did distract your men so they could make their escape."

The Chief leaned back in his chair and folded his hands in his lap. "Why?"

"Do you remember Joe Mckilligin?" Marshal asked.

"The sergeant from Frankford?"

"Yes. Joe worked very closely with Roper and learned a lot about him. When Roper showed up here in town, Joe called me and asked me to keep an eye out for him. He wasn't doing anything really, just talking to the locals. I never got around to contacting him like Joe asked me to. The bulletin about Roper kidnapping the girl wasn't on the news five minutes before I got another call from Joe. He told me I had to give the kid another chance."

"Why is Joe so interested in him?" the Chief asked skeptically.

"He said that if we brand Roper as a criminal and drive him away with this guilt on his conscience, we will make him become what we are accusing him of being."

"So you figured you would let him go so he wouldn't get sore and try to kill us all?" Hank asked.

"No, his partner asked me to give him another chance."

"I assume you are referring to Mr. Curr?" the Chief looked amused.

Marshal smiled. "Benjamin promised Roper would make it right, and honestly, I believe him. We can't get anywhere near Kora Black, but I have a feeling that with Benjamin's connections and Roper's invincibility, they will find a way."

"So you are asking the Chief to give him a chance to undo what he has done because we don't want to hurt his ego and make him turn crook?" Hank was not impressed.

"Chief, I am willing to take full responsibility for whatever Roper does in the next twenty-four hours." Marshal held the Chief's gaze.

"Seems you have a lot of faith in this kid."

"I really think he will fix this." Marshal thought of the limp body he had carried to his car that night, and prayed he was doing the right thing.

The Chief rose and went to the window. After a few minutes of silent thought he turned to Marshal. "If we can clear this up without losing men I'd rather go that route. I want you to get in contact with Roper and work out a compromise. I'll call off the search for twenty four hours."

Marshal rose quickly. "I'll see what I can do."

NINETEEN

Benjamin tugged on the bullet proof vest he wore. "This thing is not very comfortable."

"It's more comfortable than dying." Jason put the last bullet into the clip he held. He had changed out of his thrift shop disguise and washed the glue out of his hair so Benjamin could stop laughing and focus on their mission.

"Are we all on the same page on all this?" Eddie asked waving a hand over the papers spread across the table.

"I think so," Benjamin answered and Jason nodded in agreement.

"Are you sure this is the best way to do it?" Jason tossed the clip to Benjamin.

"Yes." Eddie was gathering up the papers and returning them to the folder. "To clear your record you need to be the one to get the girl."

"I agree with that part. It's you guys being the distraction that bothers me."

"Don't worry about it, we'll play it safe." Eddie held up his hand and waited, his head cocked slightly. In a moment he relaxed and headed for the back door. He opened it and a man strode in. He was a little taller than Eddie, and his face bore the evidence of years of living on the streets.

"Hey, Eddie," he said casually taking off his cloth hat and revealing a tangle of thick brown hair.

"Slaider, this is Roper and Benjamin."

"Pleasure, I've heard a lot about you." He turned to Eddie. "I've got some news for you."

"Yeah?"

"The cops called off the search for twenty-four hours."

"What do you mean?" Jason asked with a frown.

"What do I mean? Um..." Slaider glanced at Eddie "It means they aren't going to be searching for you for twenty-four hours."

"Did they say why?" Benjamin asked.

"Yeah. They're giving you time to get the girl from Maldolf." Slaider replaced his hat. "I've got to run, man. Good news, good luck." He grinned, tipped his hat and disappeared out the door.

"Well, this certainly makes things easier." Eddie gathered up the last few papers and took them down the hall. He returned with Jason's backpack and set it on the coffee table. "We don't want Maldolf to know our exact arrival time but he knows it will be in the next twenty-four. It's a little bit of a handicap, but not dodging the cops will keep things a bit more even." Eddie frowned, his eyes scanning the arsenal that was laid out on the couch. "We will have to go in light, I don't think it would be wise to take any more than these."

Benjamin picked up one of the well oiled guns and ran his hand over the barrel. "This should be plenty."

"Maldolf chose a good place to hide." Eddie picked up three of the loaded clips and clicked them one by one onto his utility belt. "He can see all the streets from the tenth floor and if he plays his cards right he'll spot us long before we get to the front door. On the up side, Maldolf only has a handful of men, they have a lot of building to cover and not enough men to do it." Eddie was still gathering his weapons. "See, if he was smart he'd use his men to totally block off that floor. Or even just the entrances of the building." Eddie gave a short mirthless laugh. "The big guys don't work like that.

They get so focused on themselves and what they want that they ultimately lose it."

Benjamin grinned at Jason. "Aren't you glad Eddie's not running the crime world?"

"Hey, I'm just telling you how it is." Eddie took the recliner once more and folded his hands behind his head. "I'd bet you twenty bucks he has at least four men guarding that one girl."

"What if they move her?" Jason asked sliding his last gun into its holster.

"I've got someone watching the place, if they try to move her, he'll let us know."

"You have a pretty tight network," Jason observed.

"Toby had a lot of friends," Benjamin told him moving to the couch. "A lot of them came from out of town like I did."

"A few of us have been working on the case with Toby for years. New or old, we all want to see it closed."

Jason nodded feeling the weight of responsibility they were placing on him. "I'll do my best."

"If you can do it, you will save a lot of lives," Eddie told him seriously. "Because either way, we are going to do it tonight."

———

"You have one hour max to get to Kora."

Jason nodded.

"We will move in on your signal, and the police should arrive soon after that."

Jason nodded again, tense and ready.

"Best of luck to you." Eddie held out his hand and Jason shook it firmly.

"Be careful."

Eddie strode off to check on a few last minute details and Benjamin stuck his hand out. "God bless."

Jason grasped his hand. "You're a great friend, Benjamin.

Don't get yourself killed."

"I'll do my best to avoid that." Benjamin laughed but his eyes were serious. "I don't see how I could get killed with this tank armor on."

Jason released his hand and smiled. "Just be careful."

"Alright," Eddie returned. "You have five minutes to get to your position. The diversion should be ready in about…" he checked his watch. "Seven minutes. You need to be going in the door by the time the second shot is fired. Got it?"

"Yes," Jason answered.

"Good, go to it."

Jason strode toward the corner of the building they were stationed behind. It was one block from the high-rise Maldolf had chosen as his hideout. It was a central building and Jason guessed he was still hoping Kora would talk in time for him to retrieve the formula. He approached the building in a wide arch as Eddie had instructed and then stopped beneath the awning of a gift shop. If Eddie's men had done their job the side door would be open. He waited, counting down the minutes as they passed.

A shot blasted through the stillness, echoing off the buildings around him. Jason pushed off the wall and sprinted across the street to the hotel. Dodging a decorative trash can he flattened himself against the wall. A wire protruded from the handleless emergency exit door and Jason used it to carefully pull the door open. He heard the second shot as he stepped into the stairwell.

Jason moved up the stairs to the third floor landing, his steps echoing loudly in the cement shaft no matter how slowly or carefully he walked. Opening the door as quietly as possible he slipped out into the hall. The end of the hall was flooded with a dim reddish glow from the emergency exit sign above him, and the widely spaced overhead lights did little to illuminate the long hall. Jason moved down the hall to the elevator and pushed the little arrow that pointed up. They probably already knew he was in the building so Jason saw no point in wearing himself out on the stairs. The doors opened and Jason found himself face to face with a small Mexican man.

"Get in," the Mexican ordered.

Jason glanced down at his gun and then obeyed. "Ten please."

"This is not a joke," the man told him, his dark eyes flashing with anger.

Jason nodded seriously but could not help smiling when the man pushed the tenth floor button.

"You will be sorry you came," the man told him.

Jason detected a hint of something in his voice that told him this man was not here by choice.

"I hope not."

There was a hiss of air and instantly the elevator was filled with a strong odor. The elevator jerked to a stop and the Mexican's eyes grew wide with fear. "They are poisoning me." He jabbed several more buttons but the elevator did not respond.

Jason reached up and pulled down the shiny plastic grid that covered the lights. Using the decorative chair rail as a step Jason shoved against the emergency trap door. It moved a little but did not open.

The Mexican's gun clattered to the floor as he plowed into the doors, his frantic desire to be free canceling out all rational thought.

"Save your energy," Jason told him, slamming his shoulder against the trap door. After years of idleness it refused to give way. "Get down in the corner and breathe through your shirt or something."

The man's eyes were wide and full of pain. The poison was already taking its toll on him. He pulled off his jacket and crouched in the corner holding it over his mouth and nose. Jason could hear him desperately mumbling something under his breath.

Jason slammed into the trap door once more and it gave way. Pushing the door upwards, he ignored the protesting metal hinges.

Jason pulled the Mexican to his feet. He was moving slowly but still seemed to be in control of his body. He placed his foot on the wooden edging and Jason shoved him upward. He caught the edge of the trapdoor and hung there, unable to pull himself up.

Jason ducked under the man and, grasping the soles of his work boots, stood quickly, propelling him partway through the trapdoor.

Jason watched as he weakly pulled himself through. Once he was out, Jason climbed on the molding again and pulled himself up through the trap door. His would-be captor was sitting with his head in his hands obviously in pain.

Jason found the control box and flipped the switch to inspection. Using the switches in the control box he moved the elevator slowly up the shaft toward Maldolf's hideout stopping just outside the tenth floor door. Jason leaned into the door latch, moving it slowly into the open position. He moved to his captor's side and dropped to one knee beside him.

"Things might get a bit rough. You are going to want to stay down," Jason told him, helping him to lay down on the top of the elevator.

"Why did you save me?" The man's voice was raspy. His dark eyes were questioning as he searched Jason's face for an answer. "I was supposed to kill you."

Jason shrugged. "I'm a hero. Heroes don't choose the victims, they just help them. I guess the Lord still has something for you to do."

The Mexican looked confused, but Jason did not have time to explain it any better. He stood again and faced the door. Taking a deep breath, he let it out slowly, glancing once more at the Mexican to make sure he had stayed down. Jason pried open the elevator doors.

Bullets sprayed him in an arch, ricocheting loudly in the elevator shaft. Jason looked past the automatic rifle and into the determined face of the man who held it.

"You got me," Jason observed cheerfully as if congratulating a child.

The man fumbled to reload. Fear had quickly replaced his determination.

"Now," Jason pulled out his handgun as the man emptied his second clip. "It's my turn."

Jason stepped into the hall dodging the butt of the rifle the man was now using as a club. He dodged again getting into position. In one smooth motion Jason grabbed the gun and twisted it from his hand. Stepping in close, Jason shoved his attacker against the wall and twisted the man's collar in his fist to keep him there.

"Where is she?"

"I don't know."

Jason let out an exasperated sigh. "Don't waste my time."

"I don't know where she is. Maldolf didn't tell me where he was taking her." He was scared and talking fast. Jason could see he was telling the truth.

Jason pulled him roughly toward the elevator shaft and shoved him onto the top of the elevator. "Use the switches there and get lost." Jason locked eyes with him. "If I see you again I'll shoot you."

The man nodded and stumbled over the Mexican in his haste. He searched the control box for a second before flipping the switch that made the elevator sink slowly downward into the shaft.

T<small>WENTY</small>

Jason slid the doors shut and looked around. The tenth floor was the mechanical floor. Pipes ran uncovered above him and insulation hung down where the ceiling panels had been removed. Water dribbled out through a new leak caused by the man's erratic shots, forming a puddle on the dirty cement floor.

Jason moved cautiously in the dimness. He had gone over the floor plans with Eddie but it was different standing in the dingy hallway. Once he was away from the soft splashing of the water, he paused to listen. He waited and was soon rewarded by the sound of a door opening further down the hall. Jason ducked behind a pile of badly stacked furniture. Several minutes passed before he heard it close again.

Eddie had guessed on the room they would be holding Kora in and the uncertainty bothered Jason. What if it was the wrong room? Would Maldolf kill Kora the way he had her father? Jason peered around the furniture and saw nothing. He stood slowly and walked down the long hall counting the doors as he went. Dirt and fine debris crunched beneath his shoes and he cringed at the sound. Stopping outside the 11th door, he put his ear against it. There was no sound from inside. Jason gently tried the knob. It was locked. He pulled out the master key Eddie had given him and slid it into the lock. The key turned and the door opened easily. Jason realized he had been holding his breath and let it out softly.

Roper Returns

Slipping into the room, he glanced around. A large water heater, surrounded with pipes that hissed and gurgled inside, took up a good portion of the room. Jason went to the door beside the water heater and opened it. Mops and buckets leaned neatly against the wall. Jason passed them without a glance. Listening at the door on the other side of the passage, He heard muffled voices but could not make out what they were saying.

Jason turned the knob slowly and waited. "Lord, please help this to work," he whispered.

Jason threw the door open and moved quickly into the room, covering the two men with his Glock.

"Don't move," Jason commanded.

One of them brought his gun up and expertly sent a bullet at Jason's chest.

Jason's eyes narrowed. "Drop your guns."

The man hesitated and Jason sent a single bullet through the wall a few inches from his head. "Drop your guns," Jason commanded again.

They obeyed sullenly.

"Bartlett knows you're here. If you don't clear out…"

"Don't give me that," Jason spat. "Bartlett's been dead for months. Or did Maldolf forget to tell you that he killed him?"

They glanced at one another. Jason knew they had known about, and perhaps participated in, Bartlett's murder.

"Where is Kora?"

"Maldolf will kill her before he lets you have her," the bold one sneered. "You're wasting your time."

Jason sent another bullet through the wall and they ducked instinctively. "I said, where is Kora?"

"Kora's dead."

This time Jason's bullet found its mark in the man's shoulder. He cried out and fell to the ground clutching his shoulder. The other man stood frozen as if unable to grasp what had happened.

"Don't worry, I've heard shoulder wounds heal fairly quickly," Jason told him without emotion. "But the next one might not be so convenient."

"She's in the…"

"No, Lance." The wounded man gasped and Lance fell silent.

"Make your choice, I don't have a lot of time," Jason told him.

Lance stepped away from the man on the floor. "I don't want to die, Tate." He turned his attention to Jason, his gray eyes cloudy with uncertainty. "She was in the maintenance room when we saw her last, but Maldolf could have moved her."

"Where would he move her?"

Lance glanced once more at Tate. "There is a little room behind the storage room. It is the third door from the stairs" He pointed toward the end of the building. "They might be there."

"Thank you. You might want to get your friend out of here before he loses more blood."

Lance nodded seriously but didn't move, his eyes darted from Jason's gun to his face and back again. Jason picked up their guns and kept them covered as he moved to the hall door. "I suggest using the stairs." He pulled the door closed and sprinted down the hall. He was two doors away when Dothan rose from behind a large stack of boxes. Jason dodged but he was too late. Dothan brought the thick metal pipe down with such force that it knocked Jason to the ground. Jason dropped the guns he had gained and scrambled to his feet. Dothan struck again. This time Jason managed to stay upright as he was slammed into the wall. He brought his Glock up but Dothan knocked it from his hand before he could pull the trigger. Jason stumbled back trying to distance himself from the massive man. Dothan's steel blue eyes were hard with hate, and Jason felt the now familiar dread gripping his heart. Again and again Dothan struck him. There was no pain connected to the blows, but the force of them drove Jason back, keeping him off balance and making retaliation impossible. It was all he could do to stay out of Dothan's reach. He knew if Dothan got a hold of him it would all be over. Jason groped desperately for his other gun only to have it knocked from his grasp.

"Lord, help me," Jason begged, scrambling frantically to his feet. A shot was fired from behind him and Dothan's huge form jerked backwards. Jason found his footing and quickly moved out of range. Dothan moved toward him, a dark stain was spreading slowly down his shirt. Another shot rang out and again Dothan jerked backward. His eyes, even more terrifying in death, rolled back in his head as he crumpled to the floor. Only when he was still did Jason turn to see who had come to his rescue.

Benjamin stood looking back at him. His face was deathly pale.

"Benjamin? How did you get here?"

Benjamin's breathing was unsteady and his attempt at a smile failed miserably.

"Are you alright?" Jason went to him and grasped his arm to steady him.

Benjamin nodded, unable to take his eyes from Dothan's body.

"Give yourself a minute." Jason remembered the gut wrenching feeling he had gotten when he had killed for the first time. Even if it had to be done to save innocent lives, killing was a horrible thing.

"I didn't think it would be…"

The door down the hall flew open and Jason stepped instinctively in front of Benjamin. Several bullets struck him before their attacker paused as if checking his sights and his target.

"I guess my minute is up." Benjamin's voice was still shaky, but there was not time for emotions. That would come later.

"He will keep us here all night if we let him," Jason told Benjamin. "We'll walk toward him. Stay right behind me. Anything that doesn't line up is fair game."

"Good thing I'm skinnier than you," Benjamin commented. He put both hands on Jason's back to help brace him against the impact of the bullets as they moved toward the man.

Jason ignored the comment. "Let me borrow your gun, I'll try to make this a little more even." He put his hand back and Benjamin handed it to him.

Jason sent a bullet down the hall toward the man, purposely missing him. The man dove for cover behind the stack of furniture.

They continued to steadily gain back the ground Jason had lost. As they passed Dothan's body the man behind the furniture changed his tactics. His shots were fewer but well aimed, no longer striking Jason's core. He was obviously trying hard to hit Benjamin.

"Where's Maldolf?" Jason demanded. "Why isn't he out here doing the dirty work?"

"You're wasting your time, Roper," The man yelled back. His bullet struck Jason's wrist.

"Keep your arms in, Benjamin," Jason warned. "He's gunning for you."

"Maldolf will get that formula and then the fight will be fair."

"Yeah? Does he even have the other half?" Jason asked. He sent another bullet in the man's direction and Benjamin dove out of range on the other side of the furniture.

"He knows where to get it."

"I don't think he does," Jason countered. He walked up to

the man, disregarding the bullets that pelted him and pried the gun out of his hand. The man punched him, but it was nothing compared to the force of the blows from Dothan. Jason struck back, knocking him off balance. The second blow sent the man to the ground.

"He doesn't know how to get it. It's just a bluff for power," Jason told him.

"What about your old man?" the man glared up at Jason from the floor.

"If he was really in contact with my dad he wouldn't have tried to drown me," Jason responded darkly. "My dad knows the only way to "deactivate" me. If Maldolf was in contact with him he wouldn't be trying lame attempts to knock me off."

"He'll get it," the man sneered but there was a hint of doubt in his face.

"Get on your stomach," Jason commanded pulling out a length of paracord.

The man rolled over with a little help from Jason's shoe.

"Benjamin, can you cover him?"

Benjamin stepped out and picked up the Glock Dothan had knocked out of Jason's hand earlier. "Alright."

"If he moves, let him have it," Jason told him coldly.

Benjamin positioned himself where he could watch the hall and the man while Jason tied him tightly.

Jason stood and looked down the hall.

"That door is open," Benjamin gestured with his head across the hall.

"Get out of range." Jason grabbed the shoulders of the man's jacket and pulled him toward the door.

Benjamin moved further down the hall putting the furniture between himself and the door.

Jason dropped the man and pushed the door open. The room was dark. Jason stuck his hand inside, groped for the light switch, and flipped it on. There was a body crumpled on the floor and a gun laying a few inches from the man's limp hand.

"What is it?" Benjamin asked.

"Someone's been shot in here," Jason told him. "I don't know if he was shot or shot himself."

Benjamin came to his side. "Let's get this one in there then. I don't think they will be looking in here for anyone."

Together they lifted their captive and put him out of sight around the corner.

"Just in case you get any ideas, I'll get this out of range." Jason took the dead man's gun and put it on the dilapidated tool shelf that took up most of the wall.

They pulled the door shut behind them and once more stood in the long dim hall.

Twenty-One

"Can't you give them twenty more minutes?"

Marshal looked over at the Chief.

"We told Roper he had an hour to do his thing," Eddie told him checking his watch.

The Chief looked up at the building. "I've already jeopardized this girl once by calling off the search. It is our job to bring her back."

"If Roper can do it you won't have to," Marshal pointed out.

"There have been a lot of shots fired, what if your hero is dead?"

"Can we give him twenty minutes?" Eddie asked seriously. "I've invested a lot in this mission and I really think he will pull it off."

The Chief sighed heavily. "Twenty minutes."

Eddie turned and gave someone across the street an enthusiastic thumbs up. "Alright, Roper," Eddie muttered "we've got twenty to pull this thing off."

———

Jason slammed into the door and it flew open. He quickly scanned the room. Sturdy metal shelves lined the walls and several took up the middle of the room as well. Tools and parts filled the shelves. Jason moved forward confidently. Gunshots echoed in the hall and Jason dodged through the clutter toward the door.

"Roper," Benjamin shouted as Jason emerged. "Oh, sorry, I thought you were inside." Benjamin pointed down the hall. "Maldolf's in there."

"You saw him?"

"He tried to shoot me," Benjamin answered. "That's sort of hard to miss."

"Was Kora with him?"

"I don't know." Benjamin lowered his voice. "The door opened once before, I think we are close to Kora. He's trying to get across the hall but doesn't want to damage himself in the process."

"Alright, I'll check this room. The guy I saw earlier said he thought this is where she was. You keep your eyes open and keep them over there as long as possible." Jason hesitated at the door. "Try not to get hurt."

"Right."

Jason entered the room once more, silently moving around the shelves. He was nearing the last shelf when there were shots in the hall once more. Jason waited but heard nothing more and started slowly forward again. He rounded the shelf and stopped. There was Kora. She had been gagged and tied to an old straight backed chair. There was a bruise on her cheek, and large dark circles under her eyes from lack of sleep. Her hair hung in disheveled strands around her face.

The barrel of her captor's gun rested on her temple but she did not look up. Her captor grinned evilly at Jason. "Drop your gun. I've got orders to pop her off if you try to touch her."

Jason gently laid his gun on the floor and glanced around, a small table that was littered with various food wrappers was shoved against the wall to his left. A sleeping bag, probably the guard's, was rolled up under the table. The wall behind Kora and her captor was almost completely taken up by two tall metal file cabinets. According to Eddie, the metal was thick enough to do the trick if Jason could get them in place.

"What about the formula?" Jason asked.

"You won't get it," The man spat.

"Obviously, but neither will you."

"I don't want it," Jason told him truthfully. "What good would it do me?"

The man frowned slightly for a second and then regained his tough attitude. "You can't fool me."

"Why isn't Maldolf here guarding her?" Jason asked keeping his voice even and calm. Another burst of gunfire broke the eerie silence and Jason glanced back toward the hall wishing he could be there to help Benjamin.

"That is what you thought he would be doing." The guard's crafty smile returned. "He's set up a little trap for you and your friend out there."

Jason did not let his concern show. "While you are in here getting killed for his captive? What good will the formula do you?"

He stiffened and pressed the gun harder against Kora's temple. She winced and moved away slightly to relieve the pressure. "You're not killing anyone."

Several shots were exchanged and Jason heard Benjamin's short cry of pain.

He stepped back so he could see around the shelf wall. "Benjamin?"

"I'm fine," Benjamin answered with pain in his voice. "There's too many of them, Roper."

"Keep him away," Kora's guard warned.

"Benjamin, stay over there. We've got a hostage situation," Jason told him calmly. Benjamin stepped into sight and Jason watched him out of the corner of his eye. Benjamin held up his gun and pointed to it, his face asking the question.

Jason gave him an almost imperceptible nod.

Something heavy slammed against the door and Jason glanced in that direction. Benjamin smiled and mouthed,

"Three minutes max."

Jason turned his attention back to the captor. "Now what?"

"Maldolf will be here soon," The man answered.

"Good, I have a few things to clear up with him." Jason put his hands behind his back, gripping the butt of his second gun as he leaned casually against the shelf to wait.

"Keep your hands where I can see them," the man ordered swinging his gun toward Jason. He realized what he was doing as Jason's gun came into view.

Jason shot the gun out of the man's hand and leapt toward him, grabbing him by the front of the shirt and jerking him away from Kora.

Benjamin appeared in time to see the man as he stumbled past, cradling his wounded hand. Benjamin struck him with the butt of his gun and he fell to the floor unconscious.

The door crashed open slamming into the wall behind it. Benjamin spun to cover his friend sending a bullet through the doorway.

"Benjamin, cut her loose." Jason tossed Benjamin the closed knife. He was shoving hard against one of the filing cabinets. It moved away from its twin and Jason slid into the gap using his back and knees to pry them further apart.

"Scare them for me." Jason strained against the heavy metal cabinet. Benjamin shot a couple of times to keep the men under cover before joining Jason. Together they moved the cabinets so that the space between them was lined up with the place Maldolf's men would come into view.

"Get her in." Jason sprinted past them and fired several random shots toward Maldolf and his men causing them to dive again for cover.

Benjamin grabbed Kora's arm and shoved her into the gap between the cabinets.

"Contact Eddie, we need the backup now," Jason yelled over the noise of the guns. He pulled a cell phone from his pocket and tossed it to Benjamin.

"It's no good, it's been shot," Benjamin told him. He pulled out a handgun and tossed it to Jason who caught it instinctively and shoved it into his belt.

"I'll go for them."

"No, Benjamin. We'll deal with this."

Benjamin ignored him and slid a new clip into his gun. He saluted Jason with his gun before trying the knob of the adjoining door. It turned and he pushed the door open.

Benjamin's gun barked and it seemed as if the two bullets had been shot simultaneously.

"Benjamin, wait." Jason spun in time to see Benjamin jerk back and slam into a ladder that was propped against a tall shelf of paint cans. The ladder slid to the side, crashing loudly onto the cement floor.

"Lord…" Jason could not pray, the anguish that flooded his soul threatened to overwhelm him. He suddenly knew why Benjamin had said it took more strength to trust and to care. Something struck him from behind and Jason spun and shot the man. Jason glanced back at Benjamin who had not moved, and took a deep breath, his face hard with determination. Jason rapidly shot several more bullets through the opening Maldolf had to come through, and a few more through the door Benjamin had opened.

With tears in his eyes Jason slammed the door and locked it, he could not afford to allow the enemy two entrances.

Snatching up his gun from the floor, Jason shoved it into his cargo pocket, and sent his last two bullets toward Maldolf's men before sprinting to the file cabinets. He ejected the clip, letting it fall to the ground as he slid a new one into its place.

Jason slipped between the cabinets and stuck his gun into his waistband. He quickly lifted Kora from where she crouched close to the wall. He stood facing her, uncomfortably close, and placed his palms on the wall behind her.

"Line your feet up with mine." He planted his feet about six inches apart, moving the cabinet a little to give his shoulders a little more space.

She looked at him for the first time, the hurt in her eyes cutting him to the quick.

"Yes, you were right and I totally blew it. I'm really sorry." One of his hands left the wall long enough to rake through his hair. "I know you don't trust me, but I can't get you out unless you work with me."

Using his right foot he moved her right foot so the toes of their shoes were touching. He planted his right foot once more and looked at her. She looked at him again and then placed the toe of her left shoe against his.

"Good. Now…"

"There they are."

"Jason, this is foolish. Give her to me." Maldolf's tone was commanding and Jason saw a little shiver of fear run through Kora.

"You will never get the formula, Maldolf," Jason answered. "Keep your body lined up with mine," he hissed to Kora.

She moved slightly to her left.

"So now you know all?" Maldolf asked condescendingly. By his voice Jason could tell he was staying close to the end of the shelf. "Did you're little FBI friends fill you in on all the details?"

"Whatever you do, stay lined up with me." Jason's voice was barely audible but she nodded to show she had heard. He raised his voice. "Yeah, they told me. But you still aren't getting the formula or the girl." He lowered his voice again. "If they sound like they are getting close shoot at them." He pulled out his Glock and handed it to her. "Stay behind me, just poke the gun out and pull the trigger. It doesn't matter if you hit anything or not."

"I can see I should have dealt with you differently last

time," Maldolf spat bitterly.

Someone entered the room, his breathing heavy. "Maldolf, there's cops all over the place and a group of men just broke through our blockade on the west end stairs. They're headed this way." He turned, barking commands to his men. "Spread out, cover the room. If anyone tries to get in here, let them have it." His evil gaze fell on Roper once more. "So you think you will just hold out until your friends arrive?" Maldolf's tone was threatening. "If I can't have the formula then neither can you."

A volley of bullets flew at them and Jason braced himself against the wall. He saw Kora dropping and grabbed her upper arm jerking her back to her feet. "Stay lined up," he told her desperately.

The shooting stopped and they waited as Maldolf's men reloaded. The room was growing steadily darker as the sun slid behind the buildings around them.

"The police will be here any second, Maldolf. Give it up. The formula won't help anyone."

"I'm not trying to help anyone, Roper," Maldolf answered coldly. "Unlike you, I'm not restrained by that pitiful sense of justice you cling to."

"You can't get away from justice," Jason retorted. "You will either get it here or after you're dead, but you will get it."

"The cops won't be able to help you this time," Maldolf said, ignoring Jason's comment.

"Shoot two shots straight up," Jason told Kora softly. "We need to let them know where we are."

She glanced up at him and then lifted the gun and squeezed the trigger.

"One more," Jason urged and she sent another bullet into the water-damaged ceiling tiles.

"You had better watch out, Jason." Maldolf's laugh was hard. "She wants you dead as much as I do."

"Don't listen to him, just keep shooting." Kora switched the gun to Jason's right side and pulled the trigger. Someone cried out and she gave him a horror stricken look.

"Don't think about it. Just keep shooting. They're trying to kill you."

She bit her lip and pulled the trigger again tears streaming freely down her face.

"I'm going to get you out of this." Jason promised.

She nodded without looking up.

"Lord, help me get her out." Jason begged softly.

They heard the sound of approaching footsteps in the hall, quick and purposeful.

"Kora," Jason whispered. "Stay lined up. No matter what happens."

Kora looked up at him, her eyes fearfully searching his.

"It's going to get intense, but you have to stay in control."

Someone grabbed Jason's shoulder and Kora screamed sending a bullet into Jason's middle. Jason pushed her head down and spun his upper body, slamming his elbow into the man's head. Bullets tore into the wall where Kora's head had been.

Jason pulled out his gun and shot a few rounds behind him to give himself a little space.

One of Maldolf's men cried out and dropped to his knees, the others dove for cover.

Jason turned quickly facing outward toward their attackers. "Keep your feet lined up."

He felt the tips of her shoes touch his heels. "Good, lean your back against the wall and put your hands against my back." Jason shot the first man who came into sight.

The man yelled and grasped his arm, ducking out of sight once more.

"That will keep us a little more stable." Jason went on as if nothing had happened. He knew he only had to keep her safe until reinforcements arrived

She obeyed timidly. Someone shot him from their hiding place and Jason rocked back slightly from the impact. She gave a little and adjusted to brace herself better.

"Here it goes, brace yourself." Jason sent two more shots into the drooping ceiling panel.

Rapid bursts of flame lit up the doorway and were immediately joined by the cries of the men as the bullets from the hall tore through the front half of the room. The attack ended as quickly as it started. The smoke filled room was silent except for the moaning of the wounded men.

"Roper?"

"Right here," Jason answered not moving.

Someone found the light switch and the room was flooded with blinding light.

"Where's Maldolf?"

"He's in here somewhere," Jason responded, "I'll keep her covered until you locate him."

"Alright." They spread out to search for Maldolf.

"Hey Eddie?"

Eddie turned back to him "Yeah?"

"Benjamin took a bullet. I don't know how bad it is..."

Eddie's face was serious. "Where is he?"

"Through that door. Eddie..." Jason shook his head. "Never mind."

"I got it," Eddie responded gently. "I'll let you know."

"Maldolf's here," someone called. "He's dead."

"Gather the survivors. Scriven, you take charge of getting them down to the ambulances." Scriven nodded and started giving orders to the four men that remained. Police flooded the room shouting orders and brandishing their weapons. Scriven stepped forward to brief the officers on what had happened while the rest of Eddie's men simply faded into the background and silently slipped from the room.

Jason moved to go to Benjamin, but Eddie shook his head. "I'll check Benjamin. You stay there until the last of this scum is moved out. We've worked too hard to give it all up to some lowlife who is still strong enough to lift a gun."

Jason returned to his position and watched helplessly as Eddie unlocked the door and disappeared into the other room.

T<small>WENTY</small>-T<small>WO</small>

Mrs. Black answered the door and her eyes fell on Kora. A little cry escaped her and she threw her arms around her daughter. They hugged each other tightly, and Kora seemed to melt in her mother's strong arms.

Mrs. Black looked over Kora's shoulder at Jason, her eyes full of tears. "Thank you," she whispered.

Jason nodded and turned to go. The other kids piled out onto the porch, hugging Kora and talking all at once.

Jason felt someone grab his waist and he looked down at Sammis who was hugging him tightly. "Hey, Sammis." Jason put a hand on the boy's head.

"I prayed you wouldn't get hurt," Sammis told him.

Jason bent to hug him. "That means a lot, Sammis. Thank you."

"Roper." Jason looked up to see Territ striding toward him. "Hello, Territ."

Sammis let go of Jason and stood beside his brother.

"I'm sorry for all the trouble I caused your family," Jason told him seriously.

"You did a lot more to help us than anyone else." Territ offered his hand to Jason. "Thank you for bringing Kora back."

Jason shook his hand firmly. "I didn't do it alone."

"We couldn't have done it without you."

"You're a good man, Territ." Jason released his hand.

"Thank you." Territ put his arm around Sammis' shoulder.

"Will we see you around?" Sammis asked.

"I'll be here until Benjamin is out of the hospital."

"How is he?" Territ's interest was genuine.

"He lost a lot of blood but the doctors say he will pull through," Jason answered

"Thank him for us."

"I'll do that." They shook hands once more before they turned to go.

Jason watched as they walked together back to their apartment. Smiling sadly, he thought of the family he had once had. He caught himself and shook his head slightly as if to shake the memory. Those days were past, leaving in their wake a terrible wound in his heart. Jason sighed softly and turned away. The Lord was slowly healing his heart, teaching him to trust once more.

———

"How do you feel?"

"Like I've been run over by a semi truck," Benjamin answered painfully. His face looked tan against the stark whiteness of the hospital bed but his eyes were tired and full of pain.

"You look like it," Jason agreed, looking at the IV in Benjamin's arm and the monitors that lined the edge of the bed.

"Thanks." Benjamin's lips turned up slightly. "Eddie tells me bullet-proof vests are actually bullet resistant...he should have mentioned that a little earlier in the game." He moved slightly to get more comfortable, and winced.

Jason ran his fingers through his hair. "Is there anything I can do?"

Benjamin managed a weak smile. "Get me out of here?"

Jason shook his head. "I don't think so. You just about scared me to death. I'm going to keep you out of trouble as long as possible." Jason pulled an arm chair up to the side of the bed and sat down.

"I guess we're even then." Benjamin turned his head to look at him.

Jason met his eyes. He had never had a friend better than Benjamin.

"I did a lot of thinking while I was lying there," Benjamin told him his voice growing stronger. "I thought about what you've been saying about God and all that. It's different when you're laying there dying. I thought about that pep talk I gave you about trusting people and all that."

"You were right about that," Jason told him. "It is harder, but it's worth it. There is no way I could have pulled all that off without you and Eddie and all those other guys pitching in."

"So the formula has been destroyed?" Benjamin asked weakly.

"Yes. I personally got it from the place where Toby stashed it and watched it burn."

"What about the other half?"

Jason met his eyes once more, his voice emotionless. "My dad was killed last week by a prison guard."

"I'm sorry, Roper."

"He was trying to pass his half of the formula on to a contact and apparently a guard caught him. I guess he knew it was his only chance to get it out and make the super criminal he was being paid to make." Jason looked away and ran his fingers through his hair again. "The report said my dad fought the prison guard and the guard killed him in self-defense," Jason sighed. "I wish I could have done something."

"What would you have done?" Benjamin asked sympathetically.

"I don't know. I guess that's what bothers me. I don't see any way I could have helped him get back on the right track. I'm just sorry he died without knowing…" Jason stopped again and took a minute to regain his composure. "He went to hell, Benjamin. I just wish there was some way I could have shown him what Jesus did for him, made him believe." Jason gave Benjamin a wry smile. "But it isn't something you can make someone do."

"I did it," Benjamin told him bluntly.

Jason frowned "Did what?"

"Believed," Benjamin answered. "That's what I was trying to tell you. When I was lying there dying, I realized how silly it was for me to preach to you about trusting when I was refusing to trust the one Person who would never let me down. I'd heard it all before, about how Jesus came to earth as a baby and never sinned and all that. Pious people had told me that if I "died in my sin" I'd go straight to hell, but I just shrugged them off. I'd seen the way they lived when they weren't out "spreading the gospel." I'd seen the way they treated their families and co-workers. Mckilligin was one of the first people who actually lived what they said. I'd met others that I could tell were different, like Toby, but Mckilligin wasn't like the other cops. He was firm and did his job, but I had seen him in action before you ever came to town, and I knew there was something different about him. When you said you believed that day in the hotel room, I thought it was all just another hoax, a way to cope with what had happened, and that it would wear off. But it didn't. You lived what you said, like Mckilligin did." Benjamin paused as a wave of pain washed over him.

"Do you want me to get the nurse?" Jason asked rising from his chair.

Benjamin waved him back weakly. "No, sit down. I need to finish."

Jason sunk slowly back into the chair.

"I saw you getting alone and reading your Bible and praying. I appreciated the way you spoke of God, but were not pushy with what you knew." Benjamin paused and closed his eyes and then went on without opening them. "I knew what you said was true, but it didn't hit home until that man shot me. I knew it had happened and somehow, even though I was drifting in and out of consciousness, it struck me that if I died, I was going to hell. It was like God whispered, 'Will you trust me?'" Benjamin opened his eyes and looked at Jason. "I didn't actually hear it or anything."

Jason grinned "This is amazing. I've been praying for this for so long."

"I know," Benjamin smiled feebly. "I thought you'd want to know that I said yes."

STRENGTH OF SILENCE

Eddie stayed where he was, listening. In the distance, a motor started up. He waited until it had faded before he stood. Dizziness washed over him, and he steadied himself against the counter. Still moving unsteadily, Eddie removed the floorboards and laid them aside. He heard something out front and froze. If the police caught him here, there would be no end of trouble. Moving toward the back door Eddie pushed it open. Outside, trash cans and a variety of other things littered the yard. A car motor rumbled toward him, and Eddie ran.

ROPER

Protecting his family was Jason Roper's top priority. When his identity is exposed by a bullet that should have taken his life, Roper scrambles to try to protect the ones he loves most. Only this time, it is him they are after.

The Man Behind The Melody

The unexpected death of his twin sister threw Mark into a whirlwind of change. Disowned by his stepfather, Mark set out with only one goal in mind, to get as far away from the hateful man as possible. He clung desperately to the last link with his sister, her saxophone. Wandering the streets, Mark's path crossed with a stranger who could see potential no one else could see. Mark, an unwanted orphan, was offered the chance to become more than he had ever dreamed. But could the stranger be trusted?

Carbon
An Unforgettable Adventure

Carbon slipped out of bed and turned on the light. Taking a sheet of thick drawing paper from her desk she drew the face of the man the article simply called Roper. Pulling the picture she had drawn earlier from her file box, she laid them side by side on the desk. It was little or nothing to go on. The prisoner could have been a thousand different people. She had no face to compare. Suddenly the image of the stranger in the alley came to mind and Carbon frowned thoughtfully. He was the only one who would know.

Taken by the Deep

"Must be a storm." Jeremy tried to sound confident.

"It's not a storm, Jeremy." Lydia's face was white and her voice faded into a whisper. "Please, you've got to let me go."

They didn't seem to hear her. Their eyes were riveted on the swirling water before them. It rose slowly as if the waves were standing, then moved forward with hypnotic swiftness.

Lydia screamed as the waters dove toward them. The salty spray wrapped around her, wrenching her from their grasp and pulling her into its depth.

THE STRIKER OF CHOI

The health of the Striker is the health of Choi. If he goes hungry, the town of Choi will grow hungry. If he is injured, the townspeople will suffer injury. He must be protected at all costs and must never leave the town of his birth. If he were to leave, the curse of the town would be in the hands of strangers.

Striker knew the legend well, but was there more to the legend than he had been told?

IN VISIBLE FEAR

Billy dropped back on the bed, flickering between the visible world and the invisible. His breathing was rapid and irregular.

"Keep quiet, Billy, and I'll do my best to keep them off your trail. They were asking about you today."

"Don't let them find me." Again, Billy grasped the man's shirt, terror in his eyes.

The dark man pried his fingers open and stepped away. "You keep your mouth shut, I'll do what I can."

Just Ordinary
And Other Stories

Is there anyone who is truly just ordinary? Step into the world of fiction where heroes face mythical enemies, wrestle against enticing deceit, and battle fierce storms in a struggle for life. Experience heartbreak, adventure, and the ultimate sacrifice as you delve into the stories of *Just Ordinary*.

www.ingramcontent.com/pod-product-compliance
Lightning Source LLC
Chambersburg PA
CBHW032211170626
46808CB00006B/2419